A CLEAN KILL

It's a busy night in Murphy's Harbour for Reid Bennett and his dog Sam, starting with the rape of a young woman, Amy Wilson, and ending with the murder of a tourist, Thad Langdon.

First it seems obvious that Langdon has been knifed and robbed by Jack McWatters, an Ojibway Indian with whom he had been brawling earlier that evening. However, when McWatters's body is trawled out of a nearby lake, it becomes clear that he has been killed by the same weapon as Langdon, and suspicion now shifts to the unknown rapist.

Evidence points to violent ex-convict Stu Oliver who has disappeared into the wilderness. But what of Thad Langdon's strange evangelical cousins, who have given Reid conflicting stories? Could one of the men taking part in the local amateur dramatic production of *A Midsummer Night's Dream*, in which Amy Wilson is also involved, be responsible for the rape, and the murder be an entirely unconnected incident?

Reid Bennett must disentangle the elements of these crimes in the face of hostility from the local council and unwelcome media interest, but he puts his own life on the line before he comes near a solution. A pacey, complex and always unexpected new mystery from one of Canada's best known crime authors.

A CLEAN KILL

Ted Wood

HarperCollins*Publishers*

To my son, Guy Lawson,
who does Reid's legal work

Collins Crime
An imprint of HarperCollins*Publishers*
77–85 Fulham Palace Road, London W6 8JB

First published in Great Britain
in 1995 by Collins Crime

1 3 5 7 9 10 8 6 4 2

© Ted Wood 1995

A catalogue record for this book is
available from the British Library

ISBN 0 00 232546 2

Set in Meridien and Bodoni

Photoset by Rowland Phototypesetting Ltd
Bury St Edmunds, Suffolk
Printed and bound in Great Britain by
HarperCollinsManufacturing Glasgow

1

The sound of the phone was like a kitten mewing. I couldn't make out the words. 'Police chief here,' I said again. 'Who's calling?'

'Amy Wilson.' She was collecting herself. 'Please help me. Please.'

'Where are you, Amy, at home?'

'Yes.' The sobs took over again and then she said, 'He, he attacked me.'

Only one type of attack causes distress like that. 'Sexually, you mean, Amy?' I tried to sound matter of fact.

'Yes,' she said. 'Please come.'

'Be right there. Three minutes. Keep on talking to my wife.'

Freda had set down the notes she had made at that night's rehearsal and was watching me anxiously. 'It's Amy Wilson, Fred,' I told her. 'Keep her talking until I get there.'

I slipped my uniform belt back on, with its holster and the .38 and went to the other phone, the unlisted line, not connected to the police office. Dr McQuaig answered and told me he'd meet me there.

Sam, my German shepherd, uncoiled from his bed under the kitchen table and trotted out with me to the car.

The Wilsons live half a mile south of us, just north of town and I was there in a minute. I let Sam out and told him 'seek' and went up and rang the bell.

Amy answered the door, her face raddled with tears, her right hand holding the ripped front of her blouse together.

I felt like a goddamn Cossack just being there but there was no choice. We don't have a woman police officer in town. I'm the whole department, me and Sam. 'Come and sit down,' I told her. 'It's over.'

Not the right thing to say. It brought on more tears. I held my hand over her back helplessly but didn't touch her. That might have freaked her right out. 'When did it happen?'

'Ten minutes ago. When I got home.' She sat down on the couch and reached out for a tissue from a fancy wooden box. She wiped her eyes with it and then sat, folding it smaller and smaller with trembling fingers.

'My dog is searching the area. If he's anywhere close, we'll find him,' I promised.

'He said he'd come back and kill me if I told anybody,' she said through clenched teeth.

'He won't. He just wanted you scared. He's that kind of creep.'

'I know what kind of creep he is!' she screeched.

'Did you get a look at him?'

'He was wearing a mask. Like a ski mask.' She had the same tight control again.

'How big was he?'

'Big,' she said, nodding so hard it became a mechanical shudder. 'He was as big as Doug.' Doug Wilson, her husband, a long-distance truck driver.

'Built strong, like Doug? Or weedy – what?'

'Strong,' she said. 'He was strong. He just grabbed me and that was that.'

'I'll get him,' I promised. It was all the help I could give. A car pulled into the drive and Sam began to bark. I went to the door and whistled him in. He bounded over and Dr McQuaig got out of his car and came up the steps, carrying his bag.

'Where is she?' He still has the soft burr of the Highlands

6

in his voice, smooth and comforting as a single-malt Scotch.

'Living room. I'll give you a few minutes, then call me in, could you?'

'Aye,' he said. 'That's best.'

He went in and I stepped down into the well-kept front yard. Everything was perfect in the moonlight, no weeds, the right mix of flowers, neat edges to the grass along the path. Amy is a city girl, like my own wife. She's a kindergarten teacher and she likes things pretty, the way Fred does. The ugliness of what had happened could crush her. I wanted to find the guy and kick him so hard he would never rape anybody else again ever. But he was gone and all I could do was to send Sam out once more, seeking. If a miracle happened, he could still be out there and I could lock him up and seal off Amy's nightmare right now, tonight.

Sam circled the area, out of my sight. He was trained to go about a quarter mile, further if he picked up a hot trail. But the rape had happened ten minutes ago. The guy could have been way out of range by now, out of town if he was in a car.

Dr McQuaig came to the door. 'Ye can come in now, Reid. The wee thing's in the bathroom.'

'Is she going to be all right?'

'She'll not be pregnant at least,' he said. 'But it'll take her a long time to get over this.'

'What happened? Was it straight rape or did he do anything else?'

'No,' he said softly. 'He raped her, but he didn't commit sodomy of any kind.'

'Thank you. Did you take a swab?'

'Aye.' He held out a small plastic bag with a ball of cotton wool in it. 'I've a felt pen here. If you'll mark it I'll take it to the office fridge an' freeze it until you can send it in.'

'Thanks again.' I squiggled my initials on the little bag

which he had sealed with Sellotape. He put it into his top pocket, not speaking. He was still not leaving.

At last he said: 'She can't stay here. The poor wee thing's terrified.'

'I'll take her home with me.'

'That'd be best. An' get her husband home if ye can.'

He strode back to his car and I tapped on the door and went back inside. Amy was still in the bathroom, I guessed, and while I waited for her I looked around the entrance hall. This is where the rape had happened. Had he left anything behind? I was hoping for something out of his pockets, a pocket-knife, keys, a wallet if fate was *really* smiling. There was nothing like that, but there was a glove, a single work-glove, stained and greasy, lying on the hallstand.

Amy came out of the bathroom, wearing a robe. She looked as if she had thrown up.

I held up the glove. 'Is this one of Doug's gloves, Amy? Or did this guy leave it behind?'

'Yes.' She nodded eagerly. 'Yes. I put it there for you. Yes. He left that behind.'

I checked it against my own hand. It would have fit me, but as I already knew he was my size, that didn't help. The smell might, though. It was rank and slimy, as if the owner worked with greasy meat. I got a plastic bag from Amy and put it inside. Then I went on with my questions.

'Can you remember anything about him? Did he have any tattoos you saw, any scars? What was he wearing?'

'No.' She sat down, crossing her legs, tucking the robe tightly around her. 'It was dark when I came in.'

'That was when it happened?'

'I'd come back from rehearsal. I was one of the last to leave. Fred had some notes for me.' I knew what she meant, my wife was directing the play she was in and I'd lived with the theatrical uproar for months, but she explained anyway. 'Some suggestions on how to say a couple of my lines, some business.' For a moment she was happy, thinking back to the intensity of her moments on stage, but then she remembered reality and shuddered.

'You drove home?'

'No. I walked, it's not far, and it's a nice evening.'
The rehearsal was at the tent they had set up on Main Street, a five-minute stroll away. 'Who was there when you left, anybody you didn't recognize?'

She shook her head. 'Your wife was there, and Carl Simmons and the stage manager and a couple of others. Carl offered to drive me home but I said no.' She bowed her head and sniffed. I waited and she went on eventually. 'So nothing was different. Nobody followed me that I could see.'

She faltered and I coaxed her, gently. 'What happened, Amy?'

She dug her hands into her lap and sat up straight. 'I came up to the porch. It was dark, like I said. And he must have been following me after all. When I got to the top step he grabbed me from behind, he put one hand over my mouth and told me: "Don't scream."'

'Would you recognize his voice if you heard it again?'

She nodded and struggled to hold on to her composure. 'He took my key and opened the door.'

'The key was on a ring?'

'No. I have a key ring but this was just the housekey, I carry it on its own when I don't take a purse with me. It slips in my pocket.'

So the guy hadn't known in advance which key opened the door, no clue there. I waited for her to continue. 'Then he shoved me through the door and pushed me down on the floor and raped me.'

This is the point where you need sexual abuse counselling training. I haven't had any so I tiptoed through the question. 'He raped you. He didn't commit any other crimes on you?'

She shook her head, eyes brimming with tears. 'Wasn't it enough, what he did to me?'

'I'll get him,' I promised, knowing it was almost certainly a lie. 'Did he touch anything other than you while he was here?'

'It wouldn't matter,' she said, suddenly intense. 'He was wearing gloves, you saw it. Work-gloves, like leather. And they smelt.' She shuddered. 'I smelt them when he put his hand over my mouth and then when he ripped my blouse. That was after he'd finished. He ripped my blouse, then he stood up and said something.'

'Can you remember what he said?'

'Yes,' she said softly. 'He said it had been a long time but it was worth the wait.'

'Did that mean anything to you? Like could this have been somebody you used to know, some guy you dated one time, before you knew your husband, somebody getting back at you?'

'There have never been any men in my life except Doug,' she said. 'And now this one.'

That cracked the shell of her control and she sobbed. I excused myself and used her phone to call home.

Fred answered and I said: 'Can I bring her over? She can't stay here on her own.'

'Of course. Are you on your way?'

'Two minutes,' I said. 'And, listen, love. This guy is on the loose somewhere. Please get that can of Mace I brought home and keep it handy.'

She laughed, but it was nervous. 'Just until the seventh cavalry get here.'

'Two minutes,' I said again and hung up. I told Amy to get a bag packed, she was coming with me. She protested but only feebly. I waited while she slipped back into blue jeans and a sweater and put some things in a bag. I was racking my brains for something productive to do. The description she had given could have included me or any of a hundred men in the area. There was nothing to go on, except for his words and the fact that he wore smelly work-gloves. It looked like a case that would never be closed.

She was still in the bedroom when the phone rang. It

rang twice while she came out to the door and looked at me, nervously. 'Pick it up,' I told her. 'If it's him, let him talk, I'll listen from the kitchen.'

She picked it up and then said: 'I'll get him.' She came to the bedroom door and said: 'It's for you. Your wife.'

I went out to the kitchen and took the phone. 'Hi, love. What's on?'

'There's trouble at the Murphy's Arms. Bradey phoned in a panic. He says two guys are wrecking the place. Can you get down there? I told him you were on a serious investigation but he's absolutely panicked. You'll have to go.'

2

Bar fights weren't uncommon at the Murphy's Arms. If Eric Bradey was panicking, things were hairy. I had to get down there. 'OK, will do, but I'll drop Amy off first. Be back in two minutes. Stay inside until I get there.'

'Rightoh.' She was working on her English accent for her own role in the play she was producing. Over the last couple of months I'd grown used to having her sound like Princess Di from time to time. Right there it made me smile, despite the situation.

Amy had her bag packed but was making noises of protest. 'It's very nice of you but you don't have to do this.'

'Wouldn't leave you here on your own, Amy. You can arrange something permanent from our place. Shall we go?'

I tried not to hurry her as she came out, locking the door carefully, but I was anxious to get down to the hotel. Bar fights are easier to understand, and solve, than rapes. I could earn fifty cents worth of my dollar that day at least by saving the place from being trashed.

Fred was waiting under the verandah light and I waved to her and let Amy out of the car, pausing only long enough to see Fred come down the steps and take her by the arm, then reversing and driving down, past Amy's house and through town.

The Murphy's Arms is below the lock, outside the town proper, at a lower level, physically and socially, than our other pub, the Lakeside Tavern which is on Main Street.

The crowd and the noise were spilling out of the front

12

door. I didn't bother struggling upstream like a spawning salmon. I went in the back way, through the stainless steel door at the rear, with Sam on my heels. It brought me in behind the beer taps where nervous little Eric Bradey was standing, nursing the baseball bat he keeps under the counter, shifting from foot to foot, plucking up his courage to step in.

He jumped when I tapped him on the shoulder, then gave a big gulp of relief. 'I called you. It's Jack McWatters an' some tourist. They must've broke a million glasses.' I went past him to the back of the crowd that was pushing, climbing on chairs, rooting for the fighters like this was a scheduled bout.

It was McWatters sure enough. He's a tall, heavy Ojibway Indian, only the word 'Indian' is not polite any more. Maybe that's what he was explaining to the other guy as the pair of them swapped big roundhouse punches and gave out grunts as if they were trying to invent their own language.

I let them go at it for a few more seconds. They were both head down, thumping one another like toys in a battery commercial. The stranger was quicker but he was lighter and McWatters had the strength of a lifetime of work in the bush. Nothing short of a chainsaw at the knees was going to bring him down.

Generally I wait until one or the other realizes he's not going to win. That halves the problem of shutting them down. One of them is glad to stand there making threatening noises instead of taking punishment. But this was shaping up to be an all-nighter so I said 'speak' and Sam sprang at them, bouncing as if his legs were springs, splitting the crowd open like a dropped melon.

The visitor let out a yell and jumped back, but McWatters only shook his head like a man coming out of the water and grabbed a beer bottle, smashing the end out on the corner of a table. Sam crouched in front of him, snarling and dodging his jab before I shouted 'fight' and he grabbed the hand that held the bottle and hung on.

McWatters roared and tried to change hands but I grabbed his left wrist and spun him around, trying to throw him. He wouldn't drop but I wasn't going to waltz around the room with him. I kicked him behind the knee and he folded like a jackknife and lay there swearing.

Sam still had his right hand. I told him: 'Drop the bottle or you're going in.'

He was sober enough to do it. Letting go of the bottle and letting himself go limp. I told Sam 'easy' and he backed off, his head lowered, eyes still fixed on McWatters's face.

'Good boy,' I told him and he gave his tail one sweep of acknowledgement.

'OK, Jack. I'm going to let you up. Go right ahead of you and sit in that chair. Don't try to take a swing at me or you're going inside. Got that?'

He nodded and I let go of his wrist and stood up, taking a careful step back out of range of a sweep kick. He's worked in bush camps with French Canadians who fight with their feet. He would have known the tricks. But he just took the couple of steps and turned around to flop in the chair. Fine. He was sober enough to go home, I judged. But still angry at the visitor. 'Wasn't for Sam I'd've punched your goddamn lights out,' he told him.

'In a pig's eye,' the visitor said. 'Eye' came out 'ah'. Kentucky, I guessed, or Virginia. He was glad to be out of the fight but too macho to let it show. I've known a hundred guys like him in the service. They have that coal-country pride. Poor they may be, but don't go thinking you're as good as they are. They've got fists and knees to prove otherwise. His face was bruised but he looked me in the eye and said: 'You must be Sam.'

McWatters slapped his knee and guffawed. The crowd snickered. 'This is Sam.' I pointed. 'I'm the police chief. What's your name and what's all this about?'

He didn't like the laughter. 'Name's Thad Langdon. I'm from Norfolk, Virginia.'

'What happened here?' I didn't really care but asking

14

the question shames people, which cools them out.

'There wasn't a whole lot to it, I guess.'

'You were taking it seriously a minute ago. What happened?'

He straightened up to his full height, eye to eye with me. 'I got me a bear this morning.'

He sounded like he expected me to reel back, awestruck. When I didn't he upped the ante. 'With a bow. From twenty yards.'

'And?' Hunters don't impress me. Not since the war.

McWatters laughed again. 'Ask 'im how he got it.'

Langdon looked around at him angrily. 'I don't live here, awright? I went with a guy knows where the bears is at.'

'Willy Veale.' He's a licensed bear operator.

'Yeah. Veale. Lives to hell an' gone in the bush.'

'He baits them,' I said. It's a crummy way to make a living. He leaves spoiled meat and fish guts around until the careful, wilderness bears get as lazy as their garbage-dump brothers. They turn up everyday for their handout. Only one day there's somebody waiting with a .308 rifle, or it's Thad Langdon with a bow that could put a bolt through a half-inch steel sheet.

Langdon was angry now. 'It's legal. Your goddamn government sold me a licence.'

'Yeah. It's legal. Fighting in here isn't. You're from out of town; where are you staying?'

'The Bonanza Motel.' He stressed the 'Mo', Southern style. 'I'm there with two cousins o' mine, Christians.'

Bradey was at my elbow now, bobbing on his toes the way short guys do when they're mad. 'Look at this place. Who's gonna pay me for all this damage?'

If that was a pitch for my support I ignored it. Civil suits are outside my job description. A cop does his best to keep the peace, or patch it up when it gets torn. Compensation is lawyer's work.

But Langdon wasn't through. If he couldn't get respect for being the mighty hunter, he would, by God, be the big spender. He pulled out a roll of American bills, thick around as his wrist and peeled off a fifty. 'There,' he said to Bradey. 'That oughta be more than you make a week outa this shithole.'

Bradey stuck the bill in his shirt pocket. 'You're banned from here,' he said. 'And you, McWatters. I don' wanna see either one o'ya in here. Got that.'

Langdon shoved his money back in his right pants pocket and picked up his coat from the floor, where his chair had tipped over. 'Fuck alla you,' he said and walked out.

McWatters stood up. He looked steady. 'How long you been here?' I asked him.

'Two beers,' he said. 'I ain't drunk. Can't you ask Eric to let me stay?'

'You heard him,' I said. He was sober, I could let him drive. 'Go home.'

He stood there a moment longer, then he said, 'You know what he done with that bear?'

I knew he was going to give me the cause of the fight and I knew that airing it would vent his anger so I went along with him. 'What did he do?'

'Left it there. All of it. Lef' it layin' for the wolves an' foxes to eat. Skinned it out and left it.' He was disgusted, at the waste and, I guessed, at the disrespect for the bear. I don't think the Ojibway have totems, the way some Western Natives do, but I happen to know that their word for bear is Mcwa. It was likely that a man called McWatters had gotten his name from the bear. Disrespect for it was like saying something bad about a guy's mother.

'That's bad, Jack. It's ignorant, but he doesn't know any better and fighting won't help. Go home. You won. It's over.'

'Ignorant,' he said. 'You're goddamn right it's ignorant.' He straightened up and walked out, still angry.

I followed him to the outer door. He didn't look back, just walked to his pickup and got in. He started it, without a lot of angry revving, and drove out quietly. I looked around but there was no sign of Langdon. That was good. I figured he'd driven off, out of harm's way, so I went back inside.

The waiters were cleaning up the confusion, sweeping the broken glass away, righting tables and bringing trays of beer. There wasn't much chance for talking, even to Bradey, who was working flat out at the beer pump, but I stood there and asked him if anybody had come in, a couple of minutes before the fight.

He couldn't remember, but Chris, one of the waiters did. He recalled a man had come in and ordered a beer just before the first table had gone over and the fight got rolling.

'Is he still in here?'

Chris looked around, frowning. 'No. Don't see him. He must've left when the fight started.'

'Didn't wait for his drink?'

'I don't see him,' he said helplessly. He had a full tray of beer and all his customers were thirsty. He could feel his tips vanishing as he stood with me. 'Can I come back?'

'Right away, this is important.'

'OK.' He skated away with his tray and unloaded. He picked up a couple more orders and was back. He laid the orders on Bradey and waited for my questions.

'What was he like; how big?'

'Tall guy.' Chris is around five-six, a lot of people look tall to him.

'Real tall, or my size?'

'You're tall,' he said with a frown as if it were a trick question. 'You're tall. I'd say he was tall as you.'

'How was he dressed?'

He pulled a disgusted face. 'You know how it is. You see a hundred people. You don't pay no special attention.'

'Has he been in here before?'

'Can't say as I've seen him around.'

'Would you know him again if you saw him?'

He thought about that, nodding. 'Yeah,' he said slowly. 'I would.'

17

'OK. Give me the best description you can right now. In the morning I'll have a guy here with a kit to make a picture of him.'

He looked surprised. 'This is important, huh?'

'Very. Now, what do you remember?'

Without an artist to interpret his thoughts, he hadn't got much. The man had been thirtyish and had a good, fit build and a full head of hair, probably black. That was it. But it was something.

'If he comes back in, call me right away. It's urgent, Chris.'

'Sure, Reid. What the hell's he done anyways?'

'I won't know until I've talked to him. Just bring him his beer and call me.'

He nodded thoughtfully, then swooped off to another table. I left and drove back on to Main Street, beyond the falls, where the bridge is, and the lock. I went into the Lakeside Tavern and checked with their help. They do mostly a dinner business but have a small cocktail bar. Nobody had come in within the last half hour. I described my suspect to Aggie on the cash register and she promised to call me if she saw him. And that was it.

Main Street runs for a hundred yards, from the bridge past the marina to the first bend in the road. From there on it resumes being a rural road. The centre of the block was taken up with the marquee that had been set up for Fred's play. It stood with its back to the marina, next to the Tavern, stretching out over half the dusty roadway. The Chamber of Commerce had erected it the day before, ready for the kickoff event of the summer. *Midsummer Night on Main Street*, a take off of *A Midsummer Night's Dream* as concocted by Fred.

My wife was in charge, producing and directing the play, and acting the role of Titania, the Fairy Queen. She had organized the whole event, including setting up a crafts sale and selling refreshments. The whole town was involved, half the women were in the play, plus a handful of men. Everyone else with anything to offer was involved

18

in some other way. It was going to be big. They'd already sold three thousand dollars' worth of tickets in advance. Big bucks for a resort town like Murphy's Harbour.

I stood there, looking at the tent and wondering if the rapist had stalked Amy from here. A lot of guys would have been fired up over the friendly excitement of the rehearsal, the stagey flirtiness of the women. They would all have looked provocative and exciting. Some guys would think it was real. They would have seen it as an invitation.

I thought about it and decided to get Fred to keep tight security in the rehearsal and for the ride home for all the cast. Maybe they could travel in convoys of cars with one of the men along to walk each of them to their house. It might not be necessary but if there was even a chance that it could prevent another rape it was worth the effort.

The only other place open was the Chinese restaurant. I checked there but they hadn't seen anyone for an hour and nobody all evening to match the limited description I gave. So I did my usual close-up chore for the night, checking all the doors on the business properties and then drove home, up past Amy's house.

On impulse I stopped there and set Sam free to seek, thinking that maybe the guy had come back to relive his moment of power. It was a good idea but it didn't work out. Sam found nothing. I gave up and drove home.

Freda was in the kitchen. She looked at my face and said: 'You didn't find him.'

'No. But there was a guy in the Murphy's Arms earlier who answers Amy's description as far as it goes, and nobody knew him. He came in at about the right time, too.'

'What can you do?'

'I'm going to get an Identikit set from the OPP and see if we can make a likeness. Then we'll find him and I'll talk to him.'

'Get him, Reid.' She unplugged the kettle and poured water into a cup. I could smell the hot chocolate. 'He's evil,' she said. 'I don't think Amy will ever get over it.'

'I'm trying, honey.'

She stirred the chocolate and picked it up. 'Be right back.'

I waited for about five minutes before she returned. She came over and sat on my lap. 'Bed,' she said and kissed my cheek. 'Get an early start and nail this creep.'

'Great idea.' She stood up and took my hand. Sam looked up at me and lowered his head as if he didn't want any part of this foolishness. He whisked under the table on to his own bed, curling down for the night. I put the light off, yawning, and followed Fred upstairs. As we reached the bedroom the phone rang.

I picked it up. 'Police chief.'

The voice was shrill with fear. 'There's a dead man on the road, Chief. I thought he was drunk but he's got blood all over him. I'm sure he's dead. Come quick.'

3

I took a deep breath. 'Where are you?'

'In my car. Just in from the highway on the south entrance to town.'

'Stay there, please. Don't touch anything. If anyone else comes by, don't let them touch anything. I'll be right there. What's your name?'

'Ernie Draper, Chief. You know me.'

'Of course. Thanks for calling, Ernie. Stay there.'

Fred was sitting up. 'What's happened?'

'There's a body on the road up by the highway.'

'Oh Reid,' she said softly and I took a moment from buttoning my shirt to kiss her. Then I finished dressing and went out, clicking my tongue for Sam. Two minutes later I was at the scene.

A couple of cars had stopped, both had their lights and flashers on and I saw two men at the shoulder of the road, staring down. I switched on the police flashers and got out with Sam.

Ernie Draper grabbed my arm. 'Thank God you're here. It's terrible. I've never seen anything so bad.' The other man nodded dumbly and then turned aside, spitting. I shone my light on the body. It was Langdon. He had tumbled sideways on to the gravel but his face was rolled up, staring open-eyed at the stars. His chest was soaked with blood.

The second man had lost his battle and he took a step away from us, shoulders heaving and threw up. I smelt stale beer. 'Keep away from the area, please,' I told him, and he scuttled across the road and finished vomiting over there.

'Was he like this when you found him?'

'Yeah. I thought it was a sacka garbage, somethin' like that. Then I saw his hand, so I stopped an' there he is.'

'Did you see anyone else? Any cars? Anything that's not here now?'

'Nothing.' He shook his head with a tight little shudder.

'Did you touch him?'

'Well, yeah. I took a CPR course one time so I felt his throat for a pulse. But he didn't have one.'

'You did right, Ernie. Thank you for calling. Can you wait here a little while, please? I need your help.'

'Glad to,' he said quickly and stood there while I knelt and played my flashlight on Langdon's face. I felt, automatically, for a pulse in his throat. There was none but the body was warm. Without touching it I checked the massive bloodstain. The whole of his front was soaked, from his chest to his feet. There was also blood in his mouth and nostrils and the front of his shirt seemed to be cut, in one place, a narrow slit just below the breastbone. A stab wound.

I stood up, moving carefully back on to the roadway, shining my light around. There was a long bloodstain, leading from about fifty feet away. It was scuffed and I could see that he had bled as he walked, dragging his feet through his own blood to the point where he had died.

The scuffs were short. He had been taking tiny, staggering steps, dying. I clicked my light off and thought. He must have been walking home. That hadn't occurred to me before. When he told me he was staying a couple of miles out of town, I'd figured he was driving. And I'd also thought the fight was over and the matter ended. But now this had happened.

I asked the men: 'Can you both come and stand behind me, please?' They did it, glancing at one another without speaking while I crouched down and spoke to Sam. 'Seek,' I told him, and he bounded away, straight to the body.

22

He stood there, barking, until I repeated the command. Then he moved off, into the low growth on the shoulder of the road and out of my sight. If the man with the knife was around, Sam would find him for me.

I asked Draper: 'Could I use your car-phone, please?'

'Sure. Help yourself.' He was still shaky but standing taller for being next to the man who had lost his cookies.

The other man said: 'Well, if you don't need me . . .' and made as if to go.

'I'd like to talk to you; could you stay here while I use the telephone?'

'Sure,' he said, his confidence coming back. I left them and sat in Draper's car to call the Ontario Provincial Police department at Parry Sound. The officer on duty was a fishing buddy and I filled him in and asked him which detectives were on duty.

'Sergeant Holland's right here. Hold on.'

Bill Holland picked up the phone. 'Hi, Reid. Letting things get out of hand, I hear.'

''Fraid so, Bill. I badly need some backup, if you can spare the time, please. Your good self, if you're not about to head home. And a uniform guy to keep the crime-scene intact until daylight.'

'I'm on till three and I'll get a car down there. How about the photographer, crime-scene guy?'

'I've got a photographer in town but I'd like it if Dave Stinson could come over when it's light and bring an Identikit.'

'You got a suspect?'

'Not for this, but we had a rape in town earlier.'

'Jesus!' He whistled. 'I'll be there soon's I can.'

He hung up and I dialled Carl Simmons, the town photographer. He picked up the phone in a blaze of Mozart. 'Hold on, please,' he said. 'I'll kill the conductor.' I waited and the music died and he came back on, his voice playful. 'Carl here. Who's this?'

'Reid Bennett, Carl. Sorry to interrupt your evening but there's been a homicide. I was hoping you could come and do the necessary for me.' His voice firmed up at once. 'Sure thing, Reid. Where are you?' I told him and he said he'd be there in five minutes.

Next call was Dr McQuaig. He was in bed but he said he'd come over and would also notify the funeral parlour to send a hearse. We don't have a morgue in town but McKenney's is always happy to oblige. I thanked him and went to my own car and took out a couple of flashing road signs and a roll of 'keep out' yellow tape.

I set up my signs at each end of the long bloodstain, outside of it, and joined them with the tape. I then extended the tape down into the bush on the side of the road. It was wet underfoot but I tied the tape to a couple of low willow bushes to make a barrier. Then I went back to talk to Ernie Draper. I flashed my light on his clothing, looking for bloodstains. If he was aware what I was looking for, he was unconcerned and even let me glance in the trunk of his car. He had no other clothing there, no bags that might have contained any. It may have seemed a touch insulting but a lot of times in homicide cases the guy who finds the body is the one who put it there. Draper hadn't. I was sure of that.

'Did anything pass you as you drove in, coming from here?'

'Nothing,' he said anxiously. 'And I didn't see anybody walking. And there weren't any headlights up ahead of me, going into town.'

I spoke to the second man who had pulled himself together now and was acting tough to compensate for throwing up. But I knew him a little, which helped cool him out. He owned a cottage up near the second lock. His name was George Todd and he said he had left Toronto at ten, which I could check if necessary and which fit his time of arrival at the scene. He wasn't happy to let me check for bloodstains but did eventually and I sent him on to his cottage.

He had just left when Sam came out of the bush, panting with exertion. I knew he had found nothing but took a few seconds to crouch and fuss him, eye to eye, thanking him for a job I could have done only in daylight and at a tenth of his speed.

Carl Simmons pulled up in his neat little Volvo wagon. He came over in a waft of cologne and I took him to the body. 'That's bad,' he said, his voice thick. 'Whoever did that knows knives and meant what he did.'

'Yeah,' I said. Carl is a gentle guy, the only obvious gay in town but I happen to know he's done time for knifing the man he suspected of killing his lover. He's tougher than he looks and a solid ally at times like this, as well as being an excellent photographer.

'I'm sorry to do this to you, Carl, but we can't leave him there all night and I need the shots.'

He recovered at once. 'No trouble, *mein Führer*. Who is he anyway?'

'A hunter, name of Langdon. I just pulled him out of a fight at the pub. He was walking back to the Bonanza.'

'Dumb idea, Mr Langdon,' Carl told the corpse. Then he asked, 'Everything, right?'

'Please. But watch where you put your feet. I haven't checked as well as I'll be able to in the morning.'

'OK,' he said crisply, and started shooting. He took a full shot of the body from every angle, then close-ups of the face, the wound, the hands, the feet. When he'd finished, and was rewinding his film, I brought out plastic bags from the police car and put them over Langdon's hands. It didn't seem likely that he would have samples of the other guy's skin under his nails, but these days forensic people solve crimes that would have baffled the hell out of Sherlock Holmes, so I did it.

It's procedure to bag his head as well but he had to be formally identified and I didn't want to freak out his cousins when I brought them in from the Bonanza.

Carl had put in a new film and he asked: 'You want some details of the bloodstains on the road?'

'Yeah. Particularly where they start, in case the other guy's footprints are in there.'

25

I was standing with him when the OPP cruiser arrived. The driver was a policewoman, Elaine Harper, who had been caught up in a case here in town the year before, the day Fred came home with the baby. She parked in the centre of the road, flashers blazing, and came down to see me. 'Hi, Reid. You sure lead an interesting life.'

'Thanks for showing up, Elaine. I'm hip-deep in alligators.'

'What needs doing?'

'Someone has to hold the fort here. I've got the ME coming, and Bill Holland. I want to talk to a man who was fighting the victim a half hour before this happened.'

'Sounds a hot priority,' she said. 'Go to. I'll keep a record of anybody who comes by.'

'Great. And I've got the hearse coming. I have to chalk the outline, in case they get here before I get back.'

She held her flashlight for me while I drew an outline of Langdon's body.

'That's good,' she said. 'Who is it you're seeing, in case the sergeant asks me.'

'An Ojibway, name of Jack McWatters.'

'Gotcha,' she said. Then dropped out of her tough cop mask to ask: 'How's Fred and the baby?'

'Just great, thanks. The baby's walking now. Fred's got her hands full.'

'Tell her "hi",' she said and waved me away.

By the time I got to the reserve it was after midnight and the place was dark. The locals don't sit around the TV set till the wee hours like city people. Jack McWatters's house was in darkness, like the rest, but his truck wasn't outside.

His wife came to the door when I knocked, sticking her face around the edge of it, obviously in nightgear. When she saw it was me she asked: 'Is Jack in trouble?'

'I just wanted to talk to him, Mrs McWatters. Has he been home?'

She shook her head. 'Said he was goin' into town for a beer.'

26

'Thank you. When he gets home would you ask him to call me? Tell him it's about what happened earlier. He'll know.'

She was completely awake now and asked: 'What is it? What's he done?'

'Don't worry. It was sorted out then, but I want to talk to him.'

She looked at me for a long time without answering. Jack was no angel. I'd been called over here once when he came in drunk and tried to bounce her off all the walls. He'd drawn probation for that but he was her husband and she was loyal. At last she said: 'All right,' and quietly shut the door.

I stood there in the darkness as a lone mosquito whined around my ear and wondered if the case were closing itself already. Had Jack McWatters followed Langdon and driven a knife into his belly? But if he had, where was he now?

4

I spent twenty minutes driving around the reserve looking for McWatters's truck. It wasn't there and I gave up and went back to the crime-scene to get his description on the air.

I wasn't happy doing it. I knew McWatters fairly well. He belonged to the broken head school of brawling. I'd never heard of his using a knife on anybody. A two-by-four maybe, but not a knife. And besides, I thought as I drove back, he hadn't been carrying a knife when he was in the bar. If he had been he would have pulled it, instead of breaking a beer bottle, when Sam tackled him.

Bill Holland had arrived by the time I got there. He was standing beside the body while Dr McQuaig crouched over it, making his examination.

They looked up at me and McQuaig said: 'That wound was meant to kill, Reid. The blade went in under the breastbone but then the hilt was pushed in against the belly so the blade pivoted upward into the heart.'

'Must have been a long blade,' I said.

'Aye.' He nodded. 'Long and narrow, a filleting knife could have done this.'

That made me update my thoughts about McWatters. All the men on the reserve lived for their hunting and fishing. There was no doubt that he owned a filleting knife, and it would be sharp enough to shave with. 'Interesting,' I said.

Holland picked that up. 'Have you found one?'

'No, but I'm looking for a guy off the reserve. He was

28

in a fight with the deceased in the hotel. He didn't have a knife with him at that time but he could have had a filleting knife with his fishing tackle in his pickup.'

'Where is he?'

'He's disappeared. I was just up to his house. I'm back to get him on the air.'

'Good,' Holland said. 'Excuse us please, Doctor.'

We went to the car and I gave the dispatcher a description of McWatters and the licence number of his truck.

'Is he dangerous?' the dispatcher asked.

'Approach with care but remember he's wanted for questioning only. There's no warrant out. I'm not sure he knifed this guy.'

I listened while he broadcast the message to the few cars he had out. Two, out of a total four in the district, were here with me. Other districts would be just as sparsely policed. There wouldn't be many people looking for McWatters.

Holland asked me: 'What have you got so far?'

'Just the fact that McWatters was in the fight and wasn't home when I got there. I didn't have him figured for a killer but he sure as hell owns a filleting knife and knows how to use one.'

The hearse pulled in from town and I went over to it. 'Thanks for coming out, Les, Joe.'

'You're welcome, Reid.' McKenney has a soft, professional voice, as if organ music should be playing in the background. His assistant pulled the gurney out of the back and trundled it down outside the crime-scene tape to the body. Carl Simmons was there and he fired off a couple of shots as we hoisted the body on to the gurney.

'Thanks, Les,' I told McKenney. 'I'll have to bring someone in to identify him in a little while. Also, I'd like to search the body before we ship it down to Toronto for an autopsy. Can you wait for me, for about an hour?'

'It shall be done,' McKenney said. I guess in his line of work you can't help sounding biblical.

29

Carl and Holland were waiting for me, Carl holding his camera case, ready to roll. 'Anything else, Reid?'

'Not that I can think of. Appreciate your turning out. When do you think I could get the shots?'

'I'll do them tonight. How does eight a.m. sound?'

'Fantastic. Thank you.'

'Good night and good hunting,' he said and left us.

Holland grinned at me. 'A little light in the loafers, is he?'

'His business,' I said. 'He's a good guy.'

He took the hint and changed the subject. 'Didn't find anything under the body. What's next?'

'I'd like to canvass in town. Ask if anybody saw a car go through.'

Holland looked at his watch. 'It's almost one.' He yawned. 'You roll up the sidewalks around around nine p.m., don't you?'

'Pretty much. The canvass has to wait until morning.'

'OK,' he said. 'Elaine can stay here and I'll be back with our crime-scene guy in the morning.' He yawned again. 'You need me with you at the funeral parlour?'

His yawn was my cue to say no. 'I can manage there. But I have to head up to the Bonanza Motel and break the news to Langdon's relations.'

'That's on my way. I'll go with you.'

'Fine. Let's cover the bloodstain first.' I brought a sheet of plastic from my car and we unrolled it over the stain, keeping it up off the surface by placing a few rocks under it and folding the plastic under them. It wasn't textbook procedure. Blood and plastic don't go well together. You should let the blood air-dry and keep it away from plastic or it goes bad. But out here I was afraid that a porcupine or a fox would find it and snuffle up all the evidence. The rules had to be bent.

Holland instructed Elaine Harper to stay at the scene and take the name of everyone who passed. It sounds like locking the stable when the horse is gone, but often the killer comes back. When I ran out of clever things to do

30

in a day or so, I would talk to everyone she had recorded.

I promised her a coffee from the all-night place on the highway and set off for the Bonanza. It's typical of roadside places all over this continent. Built in the sixties, changed hands a dozen times. Every new owner comes in with high hopes and a paintbrush, goes broke over a few years and passes it on to the next dreamer. By the emptiness of the parking area I judged there would be another new owner soon.

Holland was in his car, behind me, and I pulled up at the office and went in. There was a TV playing out back but when the manager came out he looked as if I'd woken him. He sagged slightly when he saw me. Not a customer. Damn. He rubbed his eyes. 'Yeah, Officer. What can I do for you?'

'I believe you have a party of guys from Virginia staying here?'

He didn't play games, the way some of them do, pretending to check the register cards. He just nodded. 'That's right. Three guys from Richmond, Virginia. The one who signed in was a Roy Whelan. Is something wrong?'

'I have to talk to them. Which room are they in, please?'

'Number six.' He snorted. 'My non-smoking room. Bible-bashers, I guess they are.'

'Thanks for the help.' He was bursting to ask questions but I went on out to where Holland was standing by his car, smoking. He dropped his cigarette and scuffed it out. 'They here?'

'Room six. Name's Whelan. They're cousins, Langdon told me. Born-again Christians, I think.'

'Pity,' Holland grunted. 'If they'd gone with the guy for a beer this wouldn't've happened.'

The light was on inside unit six but we couldn't hear a TV playing. Holland let me knock. He was behind me one pace, the backup eyes and ears for my meeting.

A man's voice called: 'It's open, the way you left it.'

I glanced at Holland. 'They think I'm Langdon.'

'Wrong,' Holland said. 'Try again.'

31

I knocked again and this time there were footsteps to the door and a man opened it. He was slim and short, about five-six, and looked around thirty. He had rimless glasses and was carrying a book, his finger in it to keep his place. 'You're a police officer,' he said in surprise. 'Where's Thad? Is he in some kind of trouble?'

'I'm afraid there's been a serious incident, sir. May I come in?'

He looked at me blankly and backed off, holding the door open. I stepped up into the room. Holland followed. Another man came out of the bathroom. He was taller but pale and serious, just like the one who had let us in.

'I'm Police Chief Bennett of Murphy's Harbour. This is Detective Sergeant Holland of the Ontario Provincial Police.'

'Why are you here?' The second man had a deep voice with a rounded, preacher's tone to it.

'I take it you're the cousins of a Mr Thad Langdon?'

'Yes.' The tall one nodded. 'I am Roy Whelan, this is my brother George.'

'I'm afraid I have very bad news for you,' I said. They looked at one another and then the taller one, Roy, sank to his knees and began to pray silently.

The second man said: 'Where's Thad? Why isn't he here?' His voice was a little vague. I got the impression he wasn't sparking on all cylinders, not retarded exactly, but not packing the brainpower needed for handling abstract ideas.

'I'm afraid Mr Langdon is dead.'

Now Roy stood up. There were tears in his eyes. 'We warned him not to drink. Walking along the highway in the dark. He's been struck by a car, hasn't he?'

'I'm afraid it's more complicated than that. Mr Langdon has been murdered.'

'Murdered?' The shorter man's eyes were round with horror. 'How can that be in a place like this?'

'It doesn't happen often, Mr Whelan. Perhaps with your

help I'll be able to find out why it happened and who did it.'

'Our help?' The tall one's voice had the texture of chocolate milk. 'Of course, Officer, but I don't see what we can do.'

'You may know something about Mr Langdon which will help me. But first, can I get your full names and your home address?'

The short one bent down and picked up his book. I saw now that it was a bible, with annotated margins, a working copy for a minister or a serious student. He closed it and clamped it to his chest. He frowned. 'How did you know who we were?'

'The manager told me your name.'

He looked at his brother and frowned again. Roy said: 'George gets confused easily. Is there anything I can do to help?'

'As I said, I'd like your address please, sir, then I'd like you to come with me and identify the body.'

'Of course,' Roy said in his big voice. He gave me their address and asked: 'Where is he lying?'

'I had him removed to the funeral parlour. I'd like you to come with me, right away please, for the identification.'

'Of course.' Roy went to the closet for a jacket. He gave it to his brother who laid his bible down and put on the coat, then picked up the bible again. It was his Linus blanket, I figured. He never went anywhere without it.

Roy got himself a jacket and we left. Holland tapped my arm and I turned aside to speak to him. 'You gonna check their room?'

'I'll ask when I get back with them. They'll watch me go through his stuff, you needn't wait.'

'OK,' he said. 'I'll be back in the morning.'

'Thanks, Bill. I appreciate the help.'

'No sweat.' He got into his car as I opened mine for the Whelans. I put Sam in the back and they glanced around nervously but said nothing. Holland beeped his horn shortly and drove out, turning north up to Parry Sound.

I hung a left and ran back to the Harbour. Roy Whelan said: 'You say you spoke to our cousin earlier.'

'He was involved in a disturbance. I was called in to break it up. He and the other man left the bar. He didn't tell me he was walking or I'd have driven him home.'

'That was unwise of him,' Roy rumbled.

His brother said: 'Amen', then rolled his face up to the ceiling and said: 'Lord have mercy on them for they are a righteous and a stiffnecked people.'

I kept quiet. I'm uneasy around people who advertise the fact that they're religious.

Roy leaned forward, around his brother to ask me: 'What manner of disturbance was it? A fight?'

'Yes. In a bar. Did he get into a lot of fights?'

Roy shook his head. 'Never, to my knowledge. But tell me, what happened in this fight?'

'Not a whole lot. I guess you'd score it no decision. Both of them landed some good punches but it was a fistfight, no weapons involved. And they both left afterwards. They weren't drunk so I didn't stop them going.'

'Was he in the Murphy's Arms?' George asked; there was sadness in his voice that had nothing to do with Langdon's death.

'That's right. Did one of you drop him there?'

'May the Lord forgive me, I did,' Roy said.

'What time was that?'

'At nine-thirty, thereabouts. He said he would ring the motel when he wanted to come home. I would gladly have picked him up.'

'You weren't angry that he went drinking?'

'Not angry,' Roy said. 'Saddened. My brother and I do not use alcohol in any form.'

'But you drove him to the bar?'

'Judge not that ye be not judged,' Roy said. Then he asked: 'Can you show us the spot where he died?'

'I would like to do things in sequence, Mr Whelan. First off, the identification, then I can show you the place. Then, when I drive you home, I would like to take a look at Mr Langdon's luggage, in case there's anything in it that could explain what happened.'

'What for?' George asked, but his brother made a shushing noise at him, as if he were a child.

'Very professional,' he said. 'Of course, Officer.'

The funeral parlour is just off Main Street. Most of the lights were out but McKenney had left one burning over the big double doors at the rear. I pulled in there and he had the door open before I could ring. 'Come on in, Chief.' He was whispering, as if he was afraid Langdon was going to wake up.

We went in and I told him: 'Mr McKenney, these gentlemen are Mr Roy Whelan and Mr George Whelan from Virginia. They're here to identify the deceased. Gentlemen, Mr McKenney.'

Everyone mumbled something polite and McKenney told them: 'If you'd care to wait here, please.'

He cocked his head at me and I followed him to his workroom. Langdon's body was lying uncovered. His jaw had dropped and his eyes were wide open. A thread of dried blood trailed from the corner of his mouth to his chin. The front of his shirt and light jacket were black with congealed blood. I didn't think the Whelans could handle the sight. 'Got a sheet we can throw over him, Les?'

'Of course.' He reached into a cupboard and brought one out. I guessed he'd left the body uncovered to show me how tough he was.

'OK. Let's trot him through.'

We went back to the brothers. Roy was staring at the ceiling, hands clasped. George was reading his bible. I spoke softly. 'I'm going to lift the sheet off his face, gentlemen. If you recognize this man, please put your hand on him and tell me his name.'

'Surely,' Roy said. George nodded, keeping his place in the bible with his finger.

I lifted the sheet and they both looked at Langdon's

face. Roy reached out and put his hand on the dead man's shoulder. 'This is my cousin, Thaddeus Langdon.'

'Thank you, Mr Whelan. I have to search the body and retain what I find for a day or two. The body has to go to the forensics department in Toronto. If you would like to witness the search, I'll do it now. Otherwise I can drive you and your brother home.'

'That would be best, thank you,' Roy said. George had opened his bible again and he recited aloud, without looking at the page. It was the twenty-third psalm. We waited for him to finish and McKenney said: 'Amen.' Then Roy took his brother by the arm and led him to the door.

McKenney gave me another of his whispers. 'I'll be here when you get back, Chief.'

'Thanks, Les. I'll give you the details then.'

I drove the brothers back via the southern access road, past the Murphy's Arms. Roy said: 'That's where he asked me to leave him off so he could drink.'

'That's where the fight happened,' I said, but neither of them answered and I drove on to the crime-scene.

We all got out. The Whelans went up to the crime-scene tape and looked over it at the spread-out plastic sheet. They said nothing for a long minute and then Roy spoke, his big voice cracking. 'If only I had not been so righteous. If only I had consented to go with him. I could have drunk juice, or soda.'

'Don't blame yourself, Mr Whelan. You didn't cause his death.' I paused for what my wife calls a beat, then dug in with the question. 'What manner of man was your cousin?'

'He had not given over his life to a higher power, but he was a good man,' Roy said.

'Whose idea was this hunting trip?'

'His own,' George said, and then Roy took over again. 'Thad was supposed to be coming with Walter but when Walter could not get away, he invited us to accompany him.'

'Two questions. For openers, who's Walter?'

36

'Walter is his brother, older than Thad by two years,' Roy said.

'I see. Now, did Thad ask you along for any special reason, or just for company?'

George said excitedly: 'He wanted us to see him hunt. He shot a bear from real close up with his bow and arrow.'

'It was a test of manhood he had set himself,' Roy explained. 'His brother Walter was a soldier. He served in the Gulf War, Desert Storm. He gave Thad a hard time sometimes, because he had never seen a war.'

It explained a lot. I fought alongside guys from their corner of the world. Machismo is everything there. A nice neat war could put the seal on your manhood. But without that you have to prove it. Killing a bear from thirty yards with a bow and arrow would be a good way of doing that. Either you killed him first shot or he disembowelled you while you nocked your second shaft.

'Were you with him, this morning, when he shot his bear?'

'I was,' Roy said. 'My brother George stayed at the camp.'

'And did he do well?'

Roy nodded gravely. 'I was back a little way, with the guide. The guide had a gun, in case Thad missed but Thad insisted he used it only as a last resort.'

'Did he have to use it?'

'No. Thad's first bolt went right through the bear's heart. The guide said it was a perfect shot.'

They could put that on his tombstone, I thought. Killed, and was killed, cleanly.

I had a quick word with Elaine, then drove the brothers back to the motel and asked them if I could take a look at Langdon's belongings.

'If it may help, then yes, of course,' George said.

They took me in and brought out a heavy jacket, a crossbow and quiver full of bolts and a grip.

I looked at the bow first. It was obviously an expensive

37

model with a polished butt and stock, like a rifle. One of the bolts was wrapped in foil.

'That was the one with which he killed his bear,' Roy explained. 'He was going to put it in his trophy case.'

I nodded and went through the pockets of the jacket, finding nothing but a couple of tissues and a pack of Doublemint gum. The grip, likewise, had nothing in it but clothes, including his dirty laundry which was tucked into a plastic bag from a menswear store in Norfolk.

When I'd finished my search I asked them: 'Will you notify his family? Or would you prefer for me to do it?'

'I will call,' Roy said. 'It will be easier for them to hear it from me.' No arguments there. I thanked him and left.

I stopped at the donut shop for coffee, turning down the clerk's offer of a free dozen of yesterday's slow sellers and went back and drank coffee with Elaine. She had stopped a couple of cars, but they didn't sound suspicious so I went on to McKenney's to search the body.

He opened up on the first ring and led me to his workroom where Langdon's body lay. The first thing I did was to bag the head for the forensics people, better late than never. Before I did, I checked the face one last time and I noticed there was grit on it, including what seemed to be grit in the eyes. It could have happened when he collapsed on the shoulder of the road but it looked to me as if someone had thrown dirt in his face. It's basic unarmed combat, to distract a guy with the weapon. Only he hadn't been the man with the weapon, the other guy had. One of life's mysteries.

I began going through his pockets. McKenney hovered near me, at my request, making notes on a clipboard. There was nothing in the pockets of his denim jacket so I checked his shirt. It was pasted to his chest, flat and black with blood. The pocket was empty. In his right-hand pants pocket there was a small pocket-knife, a disposable propane lighter and two eighty-seven in change.

There was no roll of bills. I stood and remembered how he had put his money away. Right hand, into the right-hand pants pocket. Only now it was empty. So was the left.

Quickly I patted him down, being extra careful around his ankles, his socks, but there was no cash there. Then I slipped off his shoes and looked inside them although I knew he could never have walked on the roll of bills he was carrying. Nothing.

McKenney asked: 'What's up, Chief?'

'His money's gone. He had a roll would have choked a horse. American money. He peeled off a fifty and gave it to Bradey for damages at the bar, I saw it.'

'And it's not there?'

'Neither is any ID. I'll check his back pocket.'

He was stiffening up now but I rolled him on to his left side and found a wallet in the right hip pocket. It was only halfway in and at an angle towards the left, as if he had reached around himself with the wrong hand to put it away. Or as if someone else had been into it and then shoved it back, against the resistance of his tight jeans.

I thought about Ernie Draper. No. He wouldn't have touched anything. I'd have trusted him with an unlocked Brinks truck. The same with McKenney.

McKenney was looking over my shoulder. 'It's not sitting right in his pocket?' he said.

'No. Either somebody's been through it since he died, or else he was just putting it back when he was stabbed,' I said.

McKenney gave a gasp of horror and I knew that he would store that little gem to pass along to the family over the bran flakes next morning.

I took out the wallet and rolled the body flat, looking closely at his stab wound. The shirt was too crusted with blood for me to make anything of it, but I wondered whether it lined up with the wound in his belly. Or was it to one side, showing that he had been stabbed while he reached around himself to put his wallet away. Either way he was just as dead, I thought sourly. What was the use of making like Sherlock Holmes?

39

His wallet was thin. It held his driver's licence, the receipt for his licence to hunt bear with bow and arrow in the province of Ontario, a MasterCard and some credit slips, mostly for gasoline on his way up here, and a few photographs.

One showed him in a tux, younger, possibly his high-school prom shot. Another was of a girl, pretty in a thin-faced way. It was signed: *All my love, Debby*. And lastly there was one of a tough-looking soldier in paratroop gear. It was inscribed: *Having a wonderful time, wish you were here. Haha.*

I replaced the pictures and set the wallet aside with his knife and lighter and the change. 'That's it, Les. I'll keep these, return them to the family. I want him to go to the Attorney-General's forensics lab in Toronto. Can you handle that for me, bill the department?'

'Glad to, Reid. Are you through here?'

'Pretty much. If you'll give me a minute to write my notes up for them, I'll be out of here.'

Ten minutes later Langdon was back in the cool room waiting an early start for Toronto and I was down the road, talking to Elaine Harper. 'Nobody's been by since you left,' she told me. 'Why don't you grab an hour's sleep. I can give you this list in the morning.'

I yawned. 'Good idea. I'll check McWatters's house first, see if he's home.'

'Then hit the sack,' she said sternly.

'Right, Mom.' I let in the clutch and drove back through town to the reserve, moving quietly, checking for his pickup.

It was not at any of the houses and nobody on the reserve has anything as fancy as a garage. A few have sheds big enough to accommodate a car but I knew that they were all filled with snowmobiles and trapping gear, they couldn't have hidden a pickup truck without a day's notice. So I drove back out of the reserve and down to the edge of the lake.

I wasn't ready to give up and go to bed, not yet. Instead

40

I set out to check the cottages around the lake to see if McWatters had gone to ground in one of them. Most of them were still unoccupied at this time of year. He could have crashed for the night in any of a hundred different houses.

The majority of the places are right on the water with a long winding driveway down to them and lots of room to park a vehicle out of sight. You can't just drive by as you could in town. But I quickly fell into the rhythm of the search: driving in through the trees, flashing the spotlight around, slapping the car into reverse and backing out. After a while it got to be as rhythmic as skipping rope or shooting skeet. The repetitions started to lull me so that I was sleepy by the time I reached the northern lock and crossed the bridge to my own side of the water. I checked my watch. It was nearly three a.m. but there were only a couple of dozen properties between the lock and my own house so I kept on.

The slope is steeper at this point on the shoreline. The driveways are all curved to minimize the gradient and the homes are grander, almost like those big summer palaces the railroad barons used to build a century ago in New England.

I covered a couple of them and then came to a really big place with the widest and best-kept driveway. I drove down, navigating three bends and stopped, thirty yards short of the big clapboard house, to shine my floodlight around. This time it glinted back at me off metal in the bush to one side of the drive. I'd found McWatters's pickup.

5

I picked up my flashlight and got out with Sam beside me. 'Seek,' I told him and he slid away into the brush. I gave him a few seconds, to make sure McWatters wasn't hiding close by, then went over to the truck and flashed my light inside the cab.

It was empty but there were dark smears on the upholstery, from the passenger side door to the centre of the seat. I studied them carefully. They looked like bad news, like someone had moved something bloody, man-handling it into the truck. Or maybe an injured man had pulled himself in, behind the wheel of the truck. Either way they had been bad news for somebody.

Without opening the door I took a careful look into the truck. There was a knife lying beside the pedals. I went around to the other door for a closer look. It was a filleting knife with a long, narrow blade worn thin by constant sharpening.

It looked as if it had been made by some hobbyist. The handle looked like mahogany but it had a hand-finished coarseness and the blade was secured through it by three copper rivets. I could imagine it had been made for Jack McWatters by some friend who was handy with tools. I looked it over but did not touch it.

Sam was rustling through the brush and then he gave a low growl. He's trained to bark if he finds somebody, to warn me and scare them. A growl meant he was puzzled. It came from down on the dock in front of the house.

I found him nosing a spot on the dock, growling and whining.

'What's up, boy?' I crouched and checked the spot. It was a stain, a faint smear, greyish brown against the green of the pressure-treated lumber. Blood.

'Could be fish blood.' I said it softly and Sam turned his big head to look at me, not keening now. 'But the owners of this place don't fish.'

I patted him and stood up. 'Seek' I told him again and urged him away up the steps from the dock. He ran off and away through the bush again while I thought. The OPP had helped me cheerfully, once. Holland had even said he would do it again, in his own good time. But for now all the favours I could muster were used up. The only helper available was Elaine Harper. I had to pull her off the other crime-scene and use her here.

While I waited for Sam to complete his search, I immobilized the truck by taking out the rotor arm and when he came back, I left him at the site with the order to 'keep', and drove back to the original crime-scene.

Elaine was out of her car, walking up and down, swinging her arms to stay awake. She stretched and yawned when I pulled up. 'Jeez. Fighting crime sure is exciting,' she said.

'It's getting that way. I've found McWatters's truck. There's a lot of bloodstains in it. Can we get that on the air, please? Also, I found a knife in the truck that might be the weapon from the Langdon killing. Can you ask the office to check if McWatters has his fingerprints on file?'

'Be better if you do it. They're bound to have questions.'

'Thanks.' I sat in her car and called the dispatcher.

He had a bunch of questions but it ended up with his promising to call Dave Stinson in early so he could come down and help. He asked if there was anything else.

'Yes, there is. I think McWatters did time for theft, about eight years back, before I got here. If he did, his fingerprints will be on file. Dave Stinson is coming out in the

morning to check the crime-scene. Can you have him
bring a copy of the prints if there is one?'

'Sure,' he said. 'If he's got a record, Dave'll have his
prints, promise.'

I gave him directions to the house where the truck was
parked and he said: 'Right. He'll be there.'

Elaine had been listening and she just asked me: 'We
going right up to the scene?'

'First I'll check with McWatters's wife, make sure he
hasn't gone home. Follow me up there, please.'

We left the crime-scene covered with its plastic and
marked by my road flashers, hoping that would deter
prowlers, either two- or four-legged, and took both our
cars up to the reserve.

McWatters's wife came to the door quickly, this time
wearing a coat over her nightclothes. I figured she was
waiting up for Jack, maybe to give him a running start
out of the door and away somewhere to hide.

She told me he hadn't come home and let me take a
quick look around inside. Everything seemed normal. The
kids were all asleep but Jack wasn't there. I thanked her,
asked her to have him call when he came in, remembering
to say 'when', not 'if'. I borrowed an old coat of his to
give Sam for the scent. Then I left and Elaine followed me
down to the place I'd found the truck.

'I want Sam to search for him,' I told her. 'If you could
stay here and watch the truck. You can stay in your car
if you like. Honk if the guy comes back.'

Elaine's a small woman to be a cop, but she's not short
of police machismo. 'I can search too,' she said. 'Don't go
pulling any chauvinist crap on me, Reid Bennett.'

'Somebody has to watch the vehicle, Elaine. I know the
terrain better than you. Sam can track him or pick up
anybody moving around better than either of us. Who
would you leave watching here?'

'OK,' she said grudgingly. 'Go for it.'

And so I gave Sam a sniff of McWatters's jacket and set
him loose. He checked the truck first, then cast around a

few feet either way, puzzled. I watched him lifting his nose from the ground, sniffing the air and the tops of the grass under the trees and then he began to feel his way down to the dock. It took him a while. Elaine was watching and she asked: 'Isn't he sure? What's the matter?'

'I'd say that McWatters was carried. That's what's baffling him. I want to see if he goes back to the dock.'

Eventually he did, finding his way down to the place he had checked earlier. The discipline of tracking McWatters had messed up his instincts, but he had come to the same conclusion. He barked at the stain and this time I fussed him and let him sniff around, seeing where his nose led him. He went to the edge of the dock, paused there a while, then drifted back to the bloodstain.

I called out to Elaine and she came down to the dock. 'What did he find?'

'See here.' I shone my light on the surface of the dock, where the stains showed brownish against the green of the lumber.

'Looks like blood,' she said.

'McWatters's blood. And Sam tracks it to here.' I pointed out the place he had sniffed. 'Makes me think somebody pulled the body into a boat, or just rolled it off the edge of the dock.'

We stood and shone our lights into the water, but the water gathered up the brightness like a white cloud about four feet down. A few small perch swam up into it but we could see nothing else. I knelt on the dock and pushed the tip of my flashlight underwater. That extended the range of our view a couple of feet but we still could not see even the weeds on the bottom.

Elaine said: 'You need a submerged light. Or a diver.'

'Yeah.' I took a slow walk around the dock, checking the mooring cleats. There were half a dozen of them, mostly without lines in them, waiting to be tied to. But on one there was a length of yellow plastic line, the standard boating line that everyone uses on the lake. Generally people seal the end with a flame, melting it down so it doesn't unravel. This cut was raw and fraying.

'Looks like somebody's cut a chunk off this one.'

I showed Elaine and she nodded. 'And did you see what McWatters has on the back of his truck?'

'Yeah, I noticed. Concrete blocks, like he was going to do some work around the house.'

'So maybe somebody tied a bunch of them on his feet and rolled him off the dock here, into the deep water?'

'I'll have to call out the divers.' I checked my watch. 'Four o'clock. Can't do it yet, they're just volunteers.'

'So, we look around some more, or what?'

'Yes. I'll walk Sam around the properties here for a while, make sure there's nobody hiding out.'

'Good. I'll watch the truck.' She went with me, back up from the dock, and I set out with Sam to check the houses all around.

We found nothing, but by the time I'd finished it was after five, a reasonable time to start calling people in an emergency like this. I checked back with Elaine and drove to the office.

My first call was to the owners of the cottage where I'd found the truck. They were an elderly couple who lived in Detroit. It made calling them a touch more difficult, Detroit doesn't set its clocks ahead in the summer like we do. In their terms, this was the middle of the night, as Cassidy told me when I rang.

'Sorry to wake you, Mr Cassidy, it's Reid Bennett, Chief of Police at Murphy's Harbour?'

'What's up? We had a break-in — what?'

'Nothing like that. But we had a homicide locally last night and I found an abandoned truck at your place. I have cause to think that a body may have been dumped around your dock.'

He gave a quick, nervous cough. 'Jesus. You can run but you can't hide. I figured that place was Shangri-la. But it's getting as bad up there as it is in the city.'

'Not really, but there's a bloodstain on your dock. Did

46

you maybe kill a fish there, last time you were up?'

'Haven't fished for years, the wife doesn't like me to.'

'That's what I thought. But my dog tracked a man there, to your dock. I have to search for the body.'

'Was our boat stolen?'

'Your cruiser's still at the dock and the boathouse is locked. Do you have a boat or a canoe that wasn't locked away?'

There was a short discussion at the other end; his wife wanted to know what was happening. He came back on. 'No, there's a rowboat and a canoe in the boathouse, but that's all.'

That was good to know, it meant the body was possibly right beside the dock. I wouldn't have to drag the whole damn lake. I thanked him and broke the news that we might need to pull a board out of his dock to test the bloodstains.

'Ah, hell.' He mumbled off the phone to his wife then came back on. 'Go ahead if it'll help your work. I'll pick up a couple of boards on my way up next time.'

I thanked him and called Wolfgang Schneider. He runs our local insurance office and is also president of the scuba club. He answered the phone on the first ring, bright and lively.

'Hi, Wolf, Reid Bennett. Hope I didn't wake you up.'

'I'm up at five every morning.' He has a deep voice and a trace of his original accent – he's as Canadian as maple syrup but he still sounds like the guys who play the only officer with a heart in those U-boat movies. He's also a fitness freak and I imagined him doing deep knee bends while he answered the phone.

'How's your day looking? I've got a serious police problem that needs your skills.'

He gave a bark of laughter. 'OK, so I know from the sweet talk I should get into my wetsuit.'

'If you could. I don't think it's going to take long,' I told him. 'I think a body has been dumped off the dock at the Cassidys' cottage. You know where that is?'

He didn't ask about the body. His side of the problem concerned him more. 'Yah,' he said slowly. 'I know the place, in front of Cassidys'. There's a hole there, along the shoreline, opposite Indian Rock. Maybe five metres deep, a hundred metres long. If he's in there, he won't go far.'

'Could you check it out for me?'

'Let me round up a couple of my guys. You going back up there now?'

'In a few minutes. I want to go by the house first.'

'Should be there in forty-five. 'Bye.' He hung up on me to start assembling his team.

There was nothing else to do at the station so I locked up and went home. Fred was up, as she usually is by six if I'm out of the house. She came to the kitchen door and kissed me. 'You must be beat?'

'A long night, with more bad news, I'm afraid.'

She looked at me nervously, afraid to ask. 'Look,' I said. 'Things are getting hectic here. I think you and the baby should head out of town for a few days, go and stay with my sister in Toronto, something.'

She poured me a cup of coffee and handed it over, acting calm. 'Can't do that, old thing. We open tomorrow night. We've got almost four thousand dollars in advance ticket sales.'

'Scrub the play,' I said. 'The hell with everything but you and Louise.' I was tired and getting angry.

She didn't argue, just asked: 'What's happened?'

'I've found evidence that a second man has been murdered.'

'Oh, Reid.' She shuddered. 'That's terrible. Two people dead?'

'One for sure. An American hunter. He's the one that the call was about last night. And now I've got bloodstains and pointers that a second guy has been killed and dumped. This time a local.'

'What are you going to do?'

'Investigate the homicides, and the rape. It's more than

48

I can handle on my own but I've got some help coming from the OPP.'

She sat down across from me, hugging her coffee cup. 'Have you got any ideas who did the killings?'

'Not any more. I thought I did, last night. But now I have to start all over again. The second victim, the missing man, is Jack McWatters from the reserve. I had him figured for the killer of the first guy.'

She had only one more question. 'Can I do anything to help?' It would be her reaction if the sky were falling.

'You're up to your eyeballs in producing the play, you must have a million things to do, surely?'

'I have more help available than you do,' she said seriously. 'If I can have half an hour on the telephone I can delegate my own problems until this evening, anyway. I have to be there at six for the dress rehearsal.'

'Well, if you could spare the time, I'd like you to stonewall the media people when they start rattling the cage. And after that, fielding the telephone calls and setting up a program for me on the office computer later on.'

She laughed. 'Now I know why you married me.'

'There are other reasons, not connected to your office skills.'

She took my empty coffee cup, resting her other hand on the back of my neck. 'I'll bet you say that to all the girls.' Then she kissed me.

I stood up and hugged her. 'When's our anniversary? I think I'm going to renew that licence for another year.'

'Chauvinist.' She took the coffee cup to the sink. 'I guess you're going right out again, are you?'

'Have to. I've got people coming in to help.'

'That's what I thought. Why don't you jump under the shower, it'll freshen you up. I'll make you a bacon and egg sandwich.'

I gave her another squeeze, *en route* to the telephone, then called Carl Simmons. He was just printing up the shots from the first killing. He whistled when I gave him the news.

49

'You think McWatters has been killed?'

'Well, it's his truck and there's blood in it, blood on the dock. It looks that way.'

'This is getting ugly, Reid. A rape and two murders. The council is going to be on your back.'

'They'll want me to call out the cavalry, do what it takes to wrap things up. I'm all for that. I've got two OPP guys coming down this morning.'

'I hate to see that,' he said. 'You know the reeve wants the OPP to take over the policing of the village.'

'Ah well. If that happens I'll retire and clip coupons.'

He snorted. 'I don't expect you have any more coupons to clip than I do. If I can help, I will. When do you need me there?'

'Should have the OPP crime-scene man here at seven. How does seven-thirty sound?'

'No problem.'

'Thanks, Carl.'

'*Di nada*,' he said and hung up.

Before I went to shower I looked in on the baby. She was sleeping, on her back with one arm thrown sideways, like something out of a painting. Her hair is a blend of my darkness and her mother's auburn. I guess you'd call it a black-gold, the kind of one-off shade that you don't see much outside of a Clairol commercial. I shut the door softly and went to shower and shave.

It freshened me up some and Fred had laid out a clean shirt so I looked presentable when I went back down. She had cooked a big breakfast and I took five more minutes to eat it there, rather than stuff it between two pieces of bread. By the time I had eaten, Amy Wilson was up and Fred kissed me goodbye and went up to ask how she was. I ducked out before I had to make conversation.

Fred had made a Thermos of coffee for Elaine and she drank it gratefully. I let her know that the scuba divers would be arriving, and that they were the good guys. Then I got out a couple of evidence bags and used one as a glove to pick up the filleting knife from inside the truck

50

and slide it into a second bag. I tagged the bag and we both initialled it and I took it and Sam back to the office.

I went into the station by the back door, which leads to the space out by my three little cells. There's a desk and two chairs. On the rare occasions I have to lock anybody up, I sit them down here to go through the formalities. It had been a month since the last drunk driver sat there and the place was clean.

I went through to the office. There's not a lot to see there either. A desk and a couple of file cabinets. A fax machine and a computer and printer that has replaced my old manual typewriter without speeding up my output much. There's a gun rack holding a Remington .308 rifle and a pump shotgun. Not very sophisticated but they, and the Smith and Wesson .38 I carry make up the entire fire power of the department. So far it's been adequate.

I went through to unlock the front door just as the OPP car pulled in and Dave Stinson got out. He's the crime-scene investigator for the Parry Sound detachment. He was in uniform, which is unusual and the first thing he did was complain about it.

'Hi, Reid. Excuse the goddamn monkey suit. Half the guys are on vacation. I'm on regular patrol duty when I'm through with you.'

'Don't worry, I'll keep you busy here all day,' I told him.

I was still carrying the knife I'd taken from McWatters's truck and he pointed at it. 'That the murder weapon?'

'Think so. I found it in the pickup truck next to the body.'

'Jack McWatters. Right?' He lifted a briefcase out of the car. 'He copped a deuce in eighty-five. Break and enter. I've got his prints here.'

'Good. I'd like you to print his truck. I figure someone else drove it.'

'What makes you think that?'

'How else would he have wound up in somebody's driveway, a mile from the first killing? It looks to me like he and some other guy mugged the first victim. It went sour and they killed him. Then they got in a fight over his money and McWatters lost. The other guy stabbed him and dumped him in the lake.'

Stinson thought about it. 'Yeah. But why did they go to that place in particular? And how did the other guy leave?'

'That, plus, who is he, is the sixty-four-dollar question. Let's go and look.'

We drove through town towards the Cassidy cottage where the truck was and I noticed a van parked outside the bait store. It had the call letters of the Parry Sound TV station on it and I groaned at the sight. The bait store was the only business open yet and I guessed the driver was inside, trying to find where the police station was located. Just what I needed, some earnest young reporter sticking a camera in my face and telling me that the people had a right to know. I put on a little more speed to get out of sight before he emerged.

We pulled into the driveway and right down to the house. Stinson got out and greeted Elaine Harper. When I joined them she asked: 'OK to take off now, Reid? You through with me?'

'Yes. Thanks for the help, Elaine.'

'No sweat.' She took out her notebook and handed me a list. 'These are all the people who stopped at the other place.'

'Great.' I glanced down it quickly. I didn't recognize all the names but she had noted an address, phone number, plus the licence of their car in case they were lying. 'I'll get on these as soon as I'm through with Dave here.'

'Look' – she stood there, awkwardly, one hand on her waist, the other on her holster. A pint-sized Annie Oakley – 'I'm working the next two days. If you still need help after that, how about I give you a hand? I'm not talking about pay duty. This is to help.'

'I'd appreciate your help, Elaine. Thank you.'

52

She waved one hand again, dismissively. 'Give me chance to see Fred and the baby.'

As she backed up the driveway, out of our sight the TV van pulled in. The woman in the passenger seat got out as I walked up to it and a moment later the driver was beside her, pointing his camera at me.

Arguing was useless. I fought a rearguard action. 'Hi. I'll give you a statement in a little while. Can you just wait here until my colleague has started his work.'

'What's he doing?' the woman asked, holding out a microphone. She was pretty in a showbiz way but her eyes were small and she compensated by using green eyeshadow that showed up fine on TV but looked tarty in the early morning sunshine.

'Please. Give me a couple of minutes and I'll bring you up to speed.' I made a little holding motion and they stood their ground, although the cameraman kept on churning.

Stinson was looking through the window of the truck. He hadn't touched anything. 'I'd like to get the photographs taken first. You want me to do it? Or are you using your local guy?'

'The local guy's on his way. If he does it he can get the prints back to us while you're doing the fingerprinting.'

'Suit yourself.' He sounded huffy.

Carl Simmons's Volvo pulled in past the TV van and came to a halt, neatly cutting off the cameraman's view of the truck. The cameraman walked sideways without taking his eye from the viewfinder until he had a fresh vantage point.

I ignored him and introduced Carl to Dave Stinson. They shook hands and Carl got out his Leica. The pair of them talked camera talk and I stood back, out of the way, and watched.

They soon decided what was needed and Carl worked quickly to photograph the bloodstains in the truck, then the one on the dock. We were standing there when I saw Wolfgang Schneider's big blue and white cruiser cutting towards us from the direction of town.

53

I waved and he pulled in, about thirty feet from shore, rocking as his wake caught up with him. 'Down here.' I pointed to the edge of the dock and he waved back. He was wearing his wetsuit with a bulky sweater over it. He had another two men with him, one in his wetsuit. The other man let the anchor out and cut the motor and Wolf and his partner put on their tanks and masks and stepped clumsily down to the diving platform at the stern. They put on their flippers, held their masks and rolled backwards together into the water.

They swam easily to the dockside and Wolfgang pushed back his mask to ask me: 'Right under here, you think?'

'Sam tracked the body here. Maybe they put it into a boat, but I don't think so; there's no boat missing.'

'OK. Down we go.' He pulled his mask down and he and his partner turned over like whales and slid under the surface. I watched the clusters of bubbles rising. Carl Simmons was taking pictures of them, using an older, smaller camera that he carried around his neck on a strap while he worked.

'These are for me,' he explained, without looking round. 'I'm putting together a portfolio of water shots. There's a pattern and a rhythm to scuba bubbles. It's amazing.'

He crouched, twisted his camera, snapping greedily until suddenly he said: 'They're coming up.'

It was Wolfgang and he pushed his mask back and gave me a thumbs up. 'Bingo!' he said. 'There's a dead man down there, tied to concrete blocks.'

6

I gave him a high sign, like he'd just scored the winning goal. 'Way to go, Wolf. Can you bring him up?'

He gave a shrug and spat water. 'He's tied down pretty solid. Concrete blocks. I can cut him loose, bring them up later if you want them.'

'That would be great. Cut in the middle of the rope and save the knots at both ends.'

'No problem.' He pulled his mask back into place and rolled head first down into the depths again, sending a quick splash of spray from his flippers.

Carl got his camera ready and we waited, watching the bubbles breaking in front of us, straining for the first glimpse of the divers. Then there was a dark tangle in the water and I could see it was both divers, pulling something big between them. And within another moment, I could make out a man's head with the paint-black Native hair that told me it was Jack McWatters.

Sam gave a low bark, then sat back when I told him easy. Carl snapped shots with both cameras, one after the other as the divers grabbed for the edge of the dock.

They held McWatters's arms up for me and I hauled him in. The body was facing away from the dock and I turned it around. The divers took his weight as much as they could and Carl helped me drag the body on to the dock, trying to keep his chest clear of the edge, protecting him from further damage.

We laid him face down on the deck and I rolled him over. The whole front of him, shirt and pants, was messy with blood, although it looked as if a lot had washed away in the water. The stain he was leaving on the deck was barely pink.

Wolfgang and his partner hung on the edge of the dock.

'Who is he?' Wolfgang asked.

'It's Jack McWatters. He was in a fight with the other victim. I had him figured for the guy who done the killing. Now he's dead as well.'

'Was he cut, what? The water was pink, there were fish all around him,' Wolfgang said.

'He's got a stab wound in the chest, the same as the other guy, the American. Looks like that killed him.'

'Same guy did it to both of them, you figure?' Carl asked as he took his close-up of McWatters's shirtfront.

'It sure looks like it.' I was distracted, examining the ties on his body, yellow plastic ropes around the neck and the ankles; the ends had been cut six inches from the body.

I asked them to bring up the weights and the divers adjusted their masks and sank again.

'What the hell's going on, Reid?' Carl asked. 'If he killed the hunter, who killed him?'

'Maybe the same guy killed both of them. The wounds are similar. We'll see.'

The divers came up, floundering under the weight they were carrying. Carl helped me take the load and we lifted the blocks on to the deck. They were ordinary concrete blocks, two to each bundle, looking like the rest of the load on McWatters's truck. They were tied together with the yellow rope from the dock.

'Those things would have kept an elephant down,' Wolfgang said. He swam around to the diving steps at the end of the dock and took off his flippers and tossed them on the dock, then hoisted himself up. He stood there, stripping off his tanks and mask while his partner got out.

I shook hands with both divers and they grinned like kids and Wolfgang asked, 'You want me to take him to town?'

I looked around, at the steep steps from the dock to

ground level beside the cottage. 'I think that would be best. But hold on a moment, please.'

I walked up to the pickup. Dave Stinson was working with his fingerprint kit. Beyond him, on the other side of the barrier, the media swarm had thickened. There were three TV cameras there, plus people with microphones covered with sponge rubber, plus a couple of still cameramen. I knew if they saw the body they would chase me to the funeral parlour; I'd have them underfoot all day.

Stinson asked: 'So what's happening, Reid. Who was in the boat?'

'Divers,' I said softly. 'They've found the owner of this truck, stabbed, weighted down, rolled in off the dock.'

He paused, his fingerprint brush in one hand, looking like an absent-minded artist. 'Want me to come down there?'

'We're going to run him back to town, unload him there, be easier, especially with those guys.' I nodded at the media people.

'For sure,' he said. 'I'll be another hour here, I'd say.'

'Then I'll see you back here. Anything you need when I come?'

'No. I'm fine.'

He turned back to his work and I went down the steps to Wolfgang. 'I'll take you up on that offer. The place is lousy with media people.'

He nodded and turned to wave at his cruiser. The man aboard had raised the anchor and was hovering off the dock. Now he backed off and made a clean approach to the dock. We all eased him in and tied the bow and stern.

'Let me get a tarp,' Wolfgang said and stepped inboard and went below. He came up with a canvas and opened it on the deck. 'Right.' He held out his hands and Carl and I lifted the body by arms and feet and got him over to the craft. The other diver joined Wolfgang, and between the four of us we eased McWatters over the side and flat on the canvas.

We lifted the scuba gear inboard and Carl said: 'OK, I'll go home. You'll have the shots later today, Reid.'

I thanked him and beckoned Sam into the boat to join me. The cruiser pulled away and headed back to the marina.

Wolfgang took over the helm, pushing the speed up. 'My cellular phone's in that blue bag,' he called out. 'You want to call somebody?'

He wanted me to use it so I thanked him and called McKenney's. Even over the roar of the motor and the wind at my end I could hear the organ music in the funeral parlour. The voice was deep and professionally sad. 'McKenney's home of rest.'

'Les. Reid Bennett here. We've found Jack McWatters. He's dead. Can you meet me at the marina with your hearse, please?'

'Where are you now? You sound as if you're in a boat.'

'Right. I'm about a mile north. We'll be there in five minutes.'

'I'll be there.'

Wolfgang, tall and rugged, was wearing his wetsuit as he steered his boat and I was surprised to realize that he was vain, anxious for his part in the drama to be obvious when we arrived at the dock. He glanced over at me and asked: 'You think the man who did this will kill again?'

I owed him for the help so I did some theorizing out loud. 'I'm starting to think this was some kind of setup. This guy must have robbed the American, maybe with the killer's help. Then they fell out over the money and the killer took him out as well.'

He sucked his teeth and altered course slightly to steer well clear of an aluminium boat full of fishermen anchored mid-channel over another pickerel spot. 'Will you catch him?'

'I sure as hell hope so. Things are going to be panicky around here until I do.'

He said no more and I stood trying to work out the sequence of the events of the night before, using the evi-

58

dence we had. The only way I could make sense of it was if McWatters and the killer had been working together. At least it gave me a line to follow. Maybe in McWatters's background I'd find a guy capable of a double killing.

I swore under my breath as Wolfgang pulled close to the marina. The street was unnaturally thick with cars and there were people all down the dock waiting for us. Wolfgang looked at me and chuckled. 'Word is out.'

'Can I see your bullhorn a moment, please?'

'Sure. Try if you like,' he said. 'It won't work. You need that dog of yours.'

I tried, booming at them. 'This is the police. Please clear the dock. Everyone off the dock.' There was some movement, the people nearest to me, at the front of the crowd, eased back a little but the people behind didn't budge and within seconds everyone had given up pretending. I could see the TV crew, the woman holding a microphone in her left hand, patting her hair with her right, the cameraman trained on our boat.

'They must have heard you talking at the cottage,' Wolfgang said. 'Picked you up on a rifle mike when you didn't know.'

'Let's hear it for technology.' I clicked on the bullhorn and tried again. 'Please clear the dock, this is police business. Please clear the dock.'

A few people backed away but the media guys hung in, right where we were coming into land. I told Sam 'speak' and he barked and snarled at them but as long as he was inboard they ignored him. As we touched in I stepped out and he followed me and barked again. People squealed with alarm but they backed up.

Some guy with a camera shouted: 'Call that dog off, we have a right.'

I raised the bullhorn. 'You are obstructing the police, would you please clear this dock. We will talk later. Thank you.'

That, plus a minute more pressure from Sam, cleared

them to the end of the dock and we were free to move the body.

We folded it into the tarpaulin and waited until I saw McKenney's hearse at the back of the crowd. He was vainly trying to get through. I raised the bullhorn again. Those things are addictive. 'Please make way for the gentleman with the stretcher.'

I had to repeat it a couple of times but eventually the crowd parted and McKenney made his way up the dock towards me, trailing his gurney.

The TV cameras were cranking and when I turned back to the boat I realized that Wolfgang was enjoying the spotlight, bulging handsomely in his wetsuit. His partner had dressed already, he was just crew. Wolfgang was the star and he was loving it. I was glad. It made it easier to ask him for a favour next time.

I ignored the crowd now that McKenney was through it and they pushed closer, one cameraman even stood up on the thwart of Wolfgang's precious boat to get a shot. Wolf, who normally wiped off every bird dropping, didn't stop him. He helped me lift McWatters's body on to the litter then stepped over the side on to the dock with it and held it up while McKenney popped the wheels down. Then McKenney and I trundled it down the dock to his hearse. Sam was at my heels and he kept the onlookers far enough back that we could work easily, sliding our load into the back of the vehicle.

'Thanks, Les. I'm through here. Can you drop me at my car?'

'Of course.' He opened the passenger side door but I held one finger up and went back to the boat.

Wolfgang was talking to the reporters, giving a modest account of his exploits. He had worked with me enough times before to know not to give away any facts that mattered. I got the attention of the other diver and asked him to keep the concrete blocks aboard the boat, I would pick them up later. He nodded and I left.

The TV woman pushed in front of me. 'Chief Bennett. Is that a second body?'

You can only stonewall so far. 'Yes, it is.'

'Is it connected with the death of the tourist who was stabbed last night here in Murphy's Harbour?'

I did what Fred recommended, smile and say as little as possible. 'I'm afraid I can't give you any information at this time. I have two cases under investigation.'

She was a bulldog. 'Can you tell us, was this person whose body you just brought in drowned?'

I cranked up the smile still further. I must have looked like a kid at Christmastime. 'As you know, I'm not a medical man, just a very busy police officer. As soon as I have some information I will be glad to share it with you. Right now, I'm afraid I have to ask you to give me some space to work in, please.'

If Wolfgang hadn't been there she would have followed me, but instead she turned back to him and I clicked my tongue for Sam to follow and went back to the hearse.

McKenney frowned when he saw I was bringing Sam but he turned and flipped a fold of canvas down for him to sit on. 'If you don't mind,' he said.

'Sure, Les. Didn't think any of your passengers would be allergic.'

That made him chuckle, a polite little hiccupping sound that he kept up until we'd reached the Cassidy place. By now there were cars parked all down the roadway and the usual mass of rubberneckers was jammed into the gateway. I got out, with Sam, thanked McKenney for the ride and made my way through the people who were pushing down to the keep-out tape, to Stinson who was putting away his gear.

'Got some good, clear prints from behind the mirror,' he told me. 'Haven't checked 'em against McWatters's yet. I'll head back to the barn, do it there.'

'Had the wheel been wiped down? The gear shift?'

'Didn't seem like it. Like I was thinking maybe he drove the truck up here himself, then somebody offed him here.'

61

'Doesn't seem likely, not with those bloodstains on the seats. You got a sample of those?'

'There was enough there to scrape a sample up.' He opened his evidence case and brought out a small glass jar. There were brown flakes and dust in it. 'That's loads for the test.'

'Good. Can you chase it off to the coroner for me?'

'Sure.' He replaced the jar and closed down the case. 'Play this right and I can keep out of the patrol car all day.'

I moved the tapes and parted the crowd for him to leave, then held my hands up for quiet and had a word with the people. 'Hi, as you can see, we've got an investigation going on here. Just so that you know, I'm working on a homicide. Now I have to leave here for a while and I'm going to ask you to stay away from the truck and the house. Will you do that for me?'

They all nodded and yessed me and I thanked them and went back for my car. I had to move the tape to get out and they all parted like good little citizens. There was one teenager in the group, a big, raw-boned redhead with a baseball cap on backwards. I figured he'd be the first to break the rules and duck through the tape, but he wouldn't do it until the crowd had thinned. With luck I'd be back by then.

McKenney was as good as his word. McWatters's body was in his examination room. He led me straight to it and offered me coffee.

He left to get it and I stood looking at McWatters's body regretfully. More than a man had been killed here. His death had killed my theory about the first murder.

I studied the body, and wondered about the spread of the bloodstains. Langdon's body had been crusted with blood within a logical radius of the wound, this blood seemed more generally spread. It was wet now, but the stain seemed to extend all the way from the knees to the chest and to involve the whole front of his clothing. The only reason I could see was that the water had made it run, like paint. I made a note to ask Dr McQuaig.

McKenney came back with the coffee. He had the cup on a tray with a bottle of Jamaica rum beside it. 'I know it's not in the rule book, Reid, but I figured you might like a little something about now.'

The rum was tempting but I knew what a gossip McKenney was. I gave him a pat on the back. 'Great idea, Les. Bad timing, that's all. When I'm through tonight I'll have a couple. Until then, thanks but no thanks.'

'You're the boss,' he said, smiling the same kind of smile I'd used on the TV woman.

I stood and gulped down the coffee while it was hot and told McKenney: 'I'm going to search the body.'

'You want me here while you search?'

'Please. I'm not expecting to find much.'

'He never had more than his welfare cheque at any time,' McKenney said with a slight sniff. 'Except when he ripped off that house one time. Chief Wallace caught him. He was the old chief.'

'Whose house was it? Someone in town?'

'Not the town proper,' he corrected me. 'No, it was a summer place up this side of the lake.'

Maybe it had been the same house where I had found his truck, and maybe that had been significant. If I ran out of things to check, I'd follow up on it.

'OK, let's see how he's fixed.' I started going through his pockets, starting with his red and black Mackinaw coat. He had a couple of fisherman's split shot in the right-hand pocket, nothing else.

In the pocket of his shirt there were a couple of five-dollar bills and in his pants pockets three dollars in change and a pocket-knife that looked like he'd carried it since he was a child. No wallet, no money-clip, nothing else. That was all he had. I took off his boots and checked in them, and his socks which were neatly darned. No money, no papers.

63

McKenney asked the obvious question. 'You think the guy who killed him took his wallet?'

'I don't know if he even carried one. I'll have to check with his wife.'

'Widow now,' McKenney corrected me smoothly. 'Not that she's going to be heartbroken at the news, from what I hear.'

'What do you hear?' I knew he'd be up to date on happenings in the white community, in town, but the reserve is a world of its own.

He shrugged. 'Oh, you know. Some of those guys on the reserve are pretty hard on their women. They keep a baseball bat behind the door and when they're drinking they tend to use it on them.'

'I've been called out twice this year to domestics on the reserve,' I told him. 'That's against about three times a month among the population at large. So, unless you want people saying you're a racist, Les, I'd cool that one.'

'As you say,' he said huffily. He picked up the coffee tray with its bottle of rum. 'If you need anything else, I'll be out front.'

'Nothing until I bring the widow in, thanks. I'll be back in a half hour.'

There was a handful of people waiting outside McKenney's, but mercifully, no media. I drove to the reserve, stopping to pick up Jean Horn before calling on the McWatters' house.

She was in her garden, setting out tomato plants. She stood up as I approached her. 'What's wrong, Reid?'

I told her and she said: 'Wait here.'

I waited, looking at the neatness of her garden. Her ancestors were growing crops for a thousand years before Columbus got here, there isn't a lot we could teach them about gardening.

When she came out again she was wearing a different sweater and shoes. It was what she wore to come into town. McWatters's wife would not need telling that I was bringing bad news.

The family was up by the time we got there. His wife was making pancakes and the kids – three of them, around five, six and seven – were sitting on the couch watching TV.

She came to the door, wiping her hands on her apron, looked at Jean and then at me without speaking.

Jean said, 'There's bad news, Irene.'

'He's dead.' It wasn't a question. She knew. 'Drivin' drunk, was he?'

'No,' Jean said. 'You want to come in and sit down?'

She didn't answer but Jean took her arm and steered her through to a kitchen chair. The kids all turned their heads to us for a moment, then back to Bugs Bunny on the TV. The sound level was deafening but I was glad of it as I crouched next to her and said, 'He was killed with a knife, Mrs McWatters.'

She looked at me, not focusing, saying nothing. Jean Horn was standing beside her and she sniffed the air, then quickly went to the stove and pulled the frypan off the heat. She flipped the pancakes and pushed it back over the burner.

Irene looked around at her, then said: 'He din't have nobody mad at him. Not that mad.'

It was the only information I would get, or would need. It meant I had to look outside the reserve for my answer to the problems.

'Thank you, Irene. I'm going to have to get somebody to identify him. I'll ask your father to do it if you'd prefer to stay with the children.'

The TV boomed into a commercial and the three children all bounced off the couch and into the kitchen. Jean Horn got three plates down from the cupboard and split the pancake three ways. 'More coming,' she said. 'Get some syrup, your mom's busy.'

The children stared at her, then went back to the couch and started eating, using their fingers.

'Wha's gonna happen now?' Irene asked softly.

'There'll be an inquest and I'll try to catch the guy who

65

did it. In the meantime, there's a couple of things to do.'

'What about me? I got three kids to feed.' She looked at me, dry-eyed. 'He had all the money. I was goin' shoppin' today. We're out of everything.'

'I'll call somebody to help,' I promised. The TV was shouting about breakfast cereal. I wanted to turn it down but there had been enough interference in their lives for one day. 'I need someone to come down and pick up Jack's truck, as well as to identify him.'

'I'll call my dad.' She went to the phone and dialled. I waited and then she spoke softly, in Ojibwa. It's a language spoken with the mouth almost closed, like Russian. I only know a few words, one of them is *tipi*, house. She used that one, then hung up.

'He's comin' now.' She stood up and took the spatula out of Jean's hands. 'I can do it.'

We went out and waited by the car until her father turned up, in his pickup. He was a tall, dignified man in his late sixties. His hair was only touched with grey despite his age. He nodded at me and went to the front door. It opened and Irene handed him out a car key, not speaking. He patted her on the arm and said something soft. She nodded and shut the door. He came to me. 'Hi, Chief.'

'Thank you for coming over, Mr Andrews. I'm sorry this has happened. Can you come with me and identify him?'

'Yeah,' he said softly. I racked my memory for any information about him. He was a friend of the Horns, I knew that much, and had served in Korea with the Canadian Army. I'd never had occasion to talk to him about any offence. A solid citizen.

Jean spoke. 'You go in Reid's car, Reg, pick up Jack's truck first. I'll walk.'

He knew she lived a couple of minutes away so he didn't waste time arguing. 'OK. Let's go,' he said.

'I'll be back later, to see Irene,' Jean told him and he nodded. I thanked her for coming with me and took off for Cassidy's.

66

We were halfway there before he spoke. He asked: 'What happened to him?'

'He was stabbed, the same way as that hunter last night. Looks like the same kind of wound, could have been the same guy did it.'

'I hear the hunter had a lot of money on him.'

'He did. But it's missing and Jack doesn't have it.'

He nodded but didn't speak again until we got to the truck. There were very few people left there by now, but the red-headed kid was one of them. I was glad we were taking the truck away. I got out with Andrews and gave him the rotor arm from the truck. He grunted and opened the hood and replaced it, checked the leads were secure and dropped the lid. I went and untied the keep-out tape. The redhead was watching me, standing off a little. I could see he was plotting trouble when I'd gone, there was an angry insolence to him. So I called him over and got his name and address.

He gave them and asked: 'Why do you need to know? What's wrong?'

'Nothing, and that's the way it's going to stay, right, Brant?'

'Sure.' He looked at me angrily, then picked up his ghetto blaster and cranked the volume up. It was hammering out some rap number and he strode away, his head jerking to the beat.

Andrews drove out, turned south towards town and waited. I retied the tape and got into my own car and followed him to McKenney's.

I left Sam in the car and went in the side door with Andrews. There was no one around so I left him in the hall on a chair and went to look for McKenney. I found him in his workroom. He had taken the body off its tarp and put a sheet over it. He and his assistant were folding the tarp. 'Ready when you are, Les.'

'I'll be right there.'

I went back to Andrews and told him what the routine would be and he nodded. Then McKenney's assistant wheeled the gurney in from the back room, I uncovered the face and he said: 'That's Jack McWatters, my daughter's husband.'

'Thank you, Mr Andrews. Could I ask you to sit for a minute, I've got a couple of things you might be able to help me with.'

He didn't say anything, just went back to his chair and sat, toying with his hat. McKenney's sidekick wheeled the gurney away again and I squatted on my heels to be at Andrews's eye level.

'What I want to know is, did Jack have any enemies who would have killed him?'

He was silent so long that I was tempted to repeat the question, but that would have been western and pushy. I waited and after about a minute he said: 'He's hit a few guys. One o' them pretty bad when he come sniffin' aroun' Irene. But nobody wanted to knife 'im.'

'How did you get on with him?'

Another long pause. 'He was bad when he drank. I talked to him one time about Irene. He gave her a black eye. He never done that again after.'

I guessed what form the conversation had taken. McWatters would have been at least as sore as his wife for a while. This was one tough man in front of me.

'There's another question. I'm not poor-mouthing Jack. I know he was in prison for a break-in but since then, since I got here, he's been clean. But' – I wagged one finger – 'the other guy who was killed was robbed. His money was taken. Now I'm wondering if Jack could have had a friend, another guy he might have worked with to roll this tourist?'

No delay this time. Andrews shook his head. 'If he'd've took that man's money he'd've done it on his own.'

'You sound pretty sure of that. Could I ask why?'

Now he paused and gave a careful answer. 'Jack din' plan things. He wanted to do somethin', he just done it.'

No help there. I thanked Andrews for coming down and turned him loose.

I went back to the station, glad to find there were no media people lying in wait for me. I put the coffee pot on and phoned the St Vincent de Paul society and the welfare department and told them about McWatters's family. The St Vincent's man said he would head over there right away with groceries. The welfare woman told me that the widow would have to come over to the office and fill out some forms. Tell me again about government assistance, I lose heart sometimes.

I poured a coffee and checked the incoming faxes. There was one from Stinson stating that the prints behind the mirror on McWatters's truck were not his, and had not so far been matched. He had shipped them to OPP head-quarters in Toronto for computer matching. He would have an answer within a day or two, if there was a match on file. He also mentioned that Holland had been delayed in court but would be coming down in an hour or so, bringing the Identikit outfit.

There was nothing else of value on the fax so I rang my home and spoke to Fred. She was on another call but got rid of them and apologized for not coming down to the station. 'It's been one panic after another. I realize now why I never wanted to be a producer.'

'Stick with it, love, it's important for the whole town. Anyway, I don't have enough reports to need computeriz-ing yet. Next week would be lots of time.'

'Are you sure? What about the media?'

'They got lots of news from Wolf Schneider – we did some diving this morning. I think they're out of our hair for a while anyway.'

'Well, if you're sure,' she said uncertainly, then: 'Oh, there's another beep. Hold on while I see who it is.'

'Listen, forget about this, you've got too much on your plate.'

'I'll come by, as soon as I can. You're a dear. 'Bye.' She hung up and I put in a call to my nominal boss, the head of the council.

We're just a village and his title is reeve, not mayor. It

ought to keep him humble, but he throws his weight around like we were the size of Chicago. It doesn't usually bother me but right now the bee in his bonnet is to fire me and let the OPP carry out the police work for the village. He claims that our taxpayers would save two thousand dollars a year, which is about what he spent last year putting new carpet into his office.

Fortunately, I've been here longer than he has and a lot of locals know that I've done a pretty good job so they're not buying. But that could change if I didn't hurry up and find the guy with the knife.

I reached him at the little garden store and nursery he runs on the highway. In a big year he would earn as much as a clerk in the government liquor store in town, but he couldn't be more proud if he ran General Motors. His wife works with him and she called him to the phone.

'Dancy here.'

'Reid Bennett. I wanted to bring you up to date on what's happening.'

'Can't this wait for the council meeting?'

'We've got a major crimewave on our hands, Ken.' He hates my using his first name. 'Last night one of the women in the play was raped. Then a man was murdered and now I've found a second man murdered the same way.'

'Good Christ!' he said and I rolled my eyes. I haven't been much on religion since Vietnam but my mother gave me a dislike of blasphemy that hasn't gone away. He spluttered inarticulately for a moment then came out with: 'What have you done?'

'I've started my investigation. It looked to me as if Jack McWatters from the reserve was the killer of the first guy. But he was the second body I found. So I guess he and the killer were in cahoots and they fought.'

'In cahoots with who?' His voice was getting tighter. I could picture the veins standing out on his forehead.

'When I know that we'll have our killer.'

He digested that for a moment then said: 'And a goddamn rape, you say?'

70

'Yes. One of the women in the cast of the play. I figure the rapist stalked her home from the rehearsal.'

'What are you doing about that?'

'I've got a lead on a guy who was in the Murphy's Arms Hotel. The OPP are bringing me down an Identikit to make a likeness and we'll circulate it. There's a good chance he's the man who did it.'

He swore again. 'Just what we need. The summer people get in town tomorrow for the play and see pictures of a rapist tacked up everywhere. They won't even stop to take their goddamn coats off. They'll be gone, up the road to somewhere safer.'

He was right on that one so I held my tongue. At last he said: 'You need the help of the OPP.'

'I've got the help of the OPP. Their crime-scene man came and dusted the pickup truck where I found the second body. A detective has volunteered to help us.' Us, not me. This was his problem as much as mine although he wasn't the guy who had to solve it.

That was the point he made next. 'Listen,' he said, with a breathless hiss in his voice. 'Listen carefully. You catch these people. The killer, the rapist. You got that?'

'It's what I'm working on.'

'Well bust your little ass on it. You hear me? Because if you haven't found the men who committed these crimes people will stay away. And if they do, you can pack your goddamn bags and leave. You got that?'

That was more than I needed. 'Cut the crap, Ken. You do your own job. And let me spell it out for you. You offer a reward, OK?'

The mention of money angered him more than the tough talk. 'Reward?' He almost screamed it.

'Fifty thousand would be good. Ten will do. For the arrest and conviction of the man who pulled these murders.'

He was raging but I overrode him. 'Because somebody knows this guy. Someone will know his patterns, his habits, how much money he's got usually and how much he's got now. They'll talk for enough money.'

71

'Listen,' he managed to squeak out.

'No, you listen. If I promise to tremble with fear because you're being nasty to me, will you get off your fat ass and chase up a reward?'

'You've done it now,' he screamed. 'You're finished, Bennett. I'll make sure of that.'

'I love you too,' I told him and hung up.

Brave talk, I told myself angrily. The hell with Dancy and the rest of the council. None of them could help me find the killer. I was just blowing off steam.

Impatiently, I stood and walked around the office. What to do next? Probably the best thing would be a canvass of the town and the properties all the way up to Cassidy's, where I'd found McWatters and his truck. That might produce something. But I also had the rapist to worry about and wanted to check the hotel with Holland, whenever he made it with his Identikit.

I checked my watch. It was after ten. Time was wasting. I went back to my desk and pulled out the special map I had made of my turf. It lists all the home and cottage phone numbers of my cottage owners site by site, all around the lake. It was custom-made for a chore like this. I could ring around the lake sequentially, carrying out my canvass in a tenth of the time it would take in the car.

There was no answer from the Andersons at the first property past the marina. I let the phone ring ten times and moved on to the next.

An hour later I had covered the whole area up to and past Cassidy's, both sides of the water. At this time of year not many people were in residence and none of them had anything to report. But at least I knew they didn't.

Holland still had not arrived and I cursed his lateness and pulled out my second map, of the few streets in town with their residents' names and numbers. Maybe one of them had been awake at midnight. But I was restless for Holland to arrive and I walked out to the front of the counter to look out of the window. And as I did so, the front door of the

72

office was tugged open, angrily, and a tall, fit-looking man in his thirties came in. 'Your name Bennett?'

'Yes.' His accent was the same as Langdon's. There wasn't a lot of resemblance except for the build but I knew at once it was the big brother, hero of the Gulf War.

I made the standard public relations speech. 'You must be here about Mr Langdon. I'm very sorry that you have to be.' It didn't soften him any.

'I'm Walter Langdon. What happened?'

'Your brother was in a fistfight in a bar in town. I broke it up and spoke to him and the man he was fighting. They left the bar. I thought your brother was driving. He was sober so I didn't interfere. It wasn't until after the incident that I learned from his cousins that he had set out to walk back. The other guy drove off in his truck.'

'Then what?' His voice was deadly calm.

'Half an hour later I got a call from a man who found him on the edge of the road. He was dead. He'd been stabbed.'

As I spoke I studied Langdon's face. It was lean and hard but intelligent. When he spoke it was softly, a voice confident of being heard. 'Who was the other guy in the fight with Thad?'

'A local man. And here's the other half of the story. I found him dead, killed the same way. It must have happened right after.'

His eyes were grey, so pale it was as if they had no irises. His face was expressionless. 'You mean you let some guy beat on my brother and then drive away. And now he's dead and my brother's dead.'

'Right.' He was churning and I set out to defuse him. 'Both of them died the same way. So you can scratch any ideas of finding the man he was fighting with. He's dead.'

He was running on empty. He must have been on the road since he got his cousin's phone call at midnight, seething with anger every mile of the way north. He wanted revenge. It was that basic. 'I want the guy's name,' he said.

'He's left a widow and three kids. I don't want you up there hassling them. They're grieving like you are.'

'Maybe I'm fixin' to bring some flowers,' he said in the same flat voice. There was a tingle in the air, the atmosphere that makes a cat's fur stand on end in the moment before an earthquake, the silence of the last moment before the shooting starts. This man was going to fight. If he couldn't fight McWatters he would be happy to fight me.

'Look. Why don't you head up to the motel and join your cousins and rest up a while?'

'You can't not give me the name.' His voice was a hiss.

'I'm in charge of the investigation. I'll be happy to help any way which won't hinder it. Giving you the information you want is likely to do that.'

He raised his voice a touch. 'Lemme speak to who's in charge in this shithole.'

'I'm in charge.'

He looked around slowly, in the same menacing way. 'What about the goddamn Mounties? Don't they run things in this piss-ass country?'

I kept it simple. 'No. If you want a second opinion you can go up to Parry Sound and talk to the Ontario Provincial Police. They'll tell you what I just told you.'

His voice sank again and he levelled his eyes at me as if they were a weapon. 'All right. Let's play this your way. Where's my brother now?'

'He was identified by his cousin and now his body has been taken to the forensic centre in Toronto for an autopsy.'

'To be split up the middle like a gutted fish? Who gave permission for that?'

'I'm sorry. It's distressing but it's standard practice. Here and in the USA.'

'What the fuck would a hick like you know about the USA?'

I ignored that and he said, 'So OK. You're gonna play dumb.' He pointed to his face. 'Take a good look at me,' he said. 'You remember me. Because I'm gonna be in your face, from now until the guy killed my brother is caught.'

74

'Your cousins are staying at the Bonanza Motel. It's about a mile north of town. You want directions?'

'What happened to my brother's stuff?'

'His belongings are at the motel. I checked his pockets and made a list of the contents.'

'Where's his money?'

'His money was gone.'

'All of it?' He stood up again, coming up to me, fists half clenched.

'When I spoke to him in the bar he flashed a big roll of bills. He gave the bar owner fifty dollars to pay for the damage done by the fight. When I searched the body the money was gone.'

'You say.' He let the words hang in the air, like a noose.

'I say.'

'He was carrying nigh on to four thousand dollars.'

'Why so much money? He wouldn't have needed more than a couple of hundred.'

'He got laid off last Thursday. That was severance money.'

'In cash, not a cheque? What kind of job did he have?'

'He worked for a computer outfit. He cashed the cheque because he figured they were going belly up. He wanted to get the cash in his hand.'

'Well, it was gone when I searched him.'

He raised a finger and wagged it in my face. 'I seen places like this back home. Some good ol' boy sheriff runs the town for what he can make. Rolls drunks. Lifts wallets on dead men. I know the way it works. Yessir. I want you to know you picked the wrong boy this time.'

He was going to take a swing at me. I could read it in his eyes and I turned half away as if I was heading for the counter. That covered my groin in case he started with his feet. I didn't know how fast he would be. 'I'll ignore what you just said. I'll put it down to your being bereaved. Why don't you go get some sleep. Come back when you're ready to talk sense.'

That was when he swung. His eyes telegraphed it and

I ducked and caught his other arm, twisting it up his back to spin him around and drive him forward three steps, head first into the wall. He struggled and swore and tried to kick so I cranked up the pressure until he stopped. 'I'm going to let you go and you're leaving. You understand?'

He was tough. He said and did nothing. He might have been dead. I kept the pressure exactly where it was, kept his face flattened sideways against the wall, blood from his nose trickling down the plaster. 'If you try to assault me again I will lock you up until this investigation is over. Do you read me?'

His eyes were scrunched up with pain and tears seeped out of the corners. 'He was my brother,' he choked out.

Behind me the front door opened. I glanced over my shoulder as Dancy came in. He looked at me and his chin dropped. 'What in the name of God are you doing, Bennett?'

'Having a discussion with this gentleman,' I said. I let go of Langdon's wrist and stepped back.

'Discussion?' Dancy almost screamed it. He was jubilant. 'Discussion? That was police brutality.'

Langdon turned around and looked at him, blood streaming down his face. 'Piss off,' he said. 'Me an' the off'cer were havin' a talk.'

Dancy swallowed and looked from one of us to the other three or four times, like some kind of mechanical doll. Then he said: 'I can't condone this. You're finished, Bennett. You're through.'

'Good,' I told him. 'But right now I've got a couple of homicides to solve. You go have a meeting or something.'

He gulped at me, wordlessly, then wagged a finger and left.

Langdon pulled a handkerchief out of his pocket and held it over his nose. 'You're in a whole lotta shit,' he said.

'Yeah,' I nodded. 'Tell me about it.'

7

Dancy slammed out to his car. I stood at the window and watched him go. Langdon stood with me, holding a bloody handkerchief to his nose. 'Had an off'cer like him in the desert.'

A minute ago he had been trying to drop me. Now he was on my side. It was an out maybe because he'd lost our fight, I didn't care, I needed allies. 'There's guys like him everywhere.' I stuck out my hand. 'Thanks for going to bat for me.'

He changed hands on his handkerchief and we shook. 'Won' make no difference. That guy's after your ass.'

'He'll have to beat off the alligators to get at it.'

Langdon laughed shortly and gave his nose another wipe. His handkerchief was overloaded with blood by now and I said: 'Come on out back, stop the bleeding.'

The only washing facility is in the cells. Each one has a sink with a cold water tap and a toilet with no seat. Langley jerked his head around questioningly when he saw them. 'Don't worry,' I told him. 'It's all the water we have.'

He went to the cell furthest from the door, furthest from me, and stood sideways to the sink as he ran the tap and sponged his face warily. Then he stuffed a piece of tissue into his nostril and dried his face. I sat on the edge of the desk and waited until he came out, dropping the wet tissues in the wastebasket, handing me back the box.

'Keep it. You may need it again.'

He put the box under his arm and stood there, uncertain what to do next now he'd swung at me.

'Do you know where the motel is, where your cousins are staying?'

'Up the highway a ways. Right?'

'Yeah. But if you're planning on breakfast, eat in town. The Deluxe Grille is better than anything up the road.'

'Where's it at?'

'On Main Street. I'm heading that way. Follow me.'

'Come on,' he said. 'I'll buy you a coffee.'

He reminded me of a Georgia cracker in my squad at Parris Island. Boot camp doesn't leave you a lot of energy for feuding, but he'd decided he didn't like Canadians. It escalated until he came at me with a bayonet. I took it off him and broke his nose with the hilt. From then on we got on fine, right up to the time I was wounded and got a dust-off out.

Langdon went ahead of me and I locked the office and got into the scout car, putting Sam in beside me in the front seat. Langdon followed me to the restaurant and we walked in together and took a booth. Lee bustled up with the coffee pot and Langdon ordered bacon and eggs over easy. We sat and sipped and I asked him: 'What are your plans?'

'I'm stayin' here until I found who killed the kid.'

'These things take time. How much time do you have?'

'The rest of my life if it takes that long.'

I set down my cup and said: 'Doing this job I've met a lot of bereaved people. They're always sad, or angry, or bitter. But you're extra angry. Care to tell me why?'

He took a gulp of coffee and set down his cup, keeping his eyes fixed on it. 'It should've been me here with him. I got a licence too, for bear. I had the time off booked. Then the air-conditioning went, on the bank.' He lifted his hands, helplessly. 'They had my boss over a barrel. He had to fix it. Had to. An' that meant me. I'm his best service guy.'

78

'So Thad came north with his cousins.'

'Pair of God-botherin' jerks.' He picked up his coffee again, in both hands. 'Lettin' him head off into a strange bar, strange town, hell, strange country, on his own.'

Now he looked up at me. 'You don't do that. Not in the service. Never. You go out, bunch of you together, so the local yokels don't get cute.'

I nodded. 'Yeah. I know.'

'How the hell would you know?' he sneered. 'You were in the goddamn service?'

'Three years' worth.'

The thought angered him, or made him embarrassed. 'Right here, in this country, right?'

'You were in the desert, I heard.'

He was careful. 'Yeah, all through Desert Storm. Where were you?'

I could have played coy with him but he needed something to believe in. I figured my service record would help him feel better. 'US Marines. Two tours in Nam.'

He looked me in the face blankly for a moment, then laughed. 'An' I figured I was gonna whip your ass.' He stuck out his hand. 'Happy to make your acquaintance. I'm Walt Langdon.'

I shook, solemnly, the way he wanted. 'Bennett. Reid Bennett. I'm the police chief and the whole department.'

'Chief it is,' he said. His smile would have fooled anybody sitting across the room, but I read it differently. His eyes were still a pair of stones.

Lee arrived with his breakfast and he looked up and nodded thanks, then offered me a piece of his toast which I refused. All traces of his anger were gone, but I was waiting for the other shoe to drop.

He ate slowly. 'Where was the fight? The one you broke up.'

'At the Murphy's Arms. You passed it, down by the water, just before you come to the bridge.'

'An' where was he killed? Was it that place with the road markers an' the plastic sheet on the road?'

'Right. I had an officer from another department guarding the site all night, until I found the truck belonging to the guy he'd been fighting with; that was around three.'

Langdon set down his fork and picked up his coffee cup. 'Who's doin' it? Got any idea?'

'Not a lot. But I'm working on it, and I've got to go. You know where you're headed after this?'

'I'll find it.' He set down his coffee cup. 'Looks to me like you'll need all the help you can get. I'll be here.'

'Yeah,' I said and stood up. 'Thank you. You give me a call at the station any time.'

'Right.'

My first stop was down the block at the bait store. Gilles Perault doesn't live there, he has a place back away from the water but I asked him if any of his customers had been out night fishing. They might have heard something. He said he would check and get them to call me. It was a long shot but I didn't have any other kind.

I checked back at the station but still Holland had not shown up. It was annoying but he was a volunteer, I couldn't pressure him. So I went to the Murphy's Arms to check with Eric Bradey. He was at the back door where a beer truck was unloading, checking his order against a list on a clipboard. I didn't approach until the truck driver rolled the back door down and climbed into his cab. Bradey noticed me then and waved me over. 'Gotta watch that guy,' he said. 'I was short a couple two-fours last week. Don't know how the hell he did it. I counted all the cases in.'

'Maybe he carted them out again, on a dolly full of empties. One full one in the middle. You wouldn't see that. As long as he told you the number of empties you were expecting you wouldn't check.'

'Sonofabitch. I never thought of that.' He looked at me with new respect. 'I'll check the empties next time. If he's doin' that, I'll have his goddamn job.'

He would have embroidered this idea for an hour but

I headed him off. 'Eric. Did you and your guys make a list of who was in here last night, like I asked you?'

'I did, an' Pete did. Me an' him talked about it after closing last night.'

'And Chris?'

'No.' He shook his head. 'Chris's wife's expectin'. He took off home right away. Said he'd bring it in today.'

'Can I look at your list?'

'Yeah. Come on in.' He led me in and shut the door behind me. We walked up the long corridor to the bar, past the beer cooler where Bradey paused to look inside and shake his head. 'Carried out with the empties. It's a good job you're not a crook, Reid.'

The place had been swabbed out the night before. It smelt like a pine forest and all the chairs were up on the tables. Bradey had a coffee pot on the bar and he waved at it. 'Wanna coffee? An eye-opener?'

I shook my head and he took a piece of paper out of the cash register which was hanging open. He held it to his chest where I couldn't see it while he explained. 'Like this was Pete's idea. He made a map of the tables. He could remember his own pretty good, but he didn't know much about Chris's. When he got stuck, I tried to help.'

Now he showed me the paper. It was covered with roughly drawn circles representing the tables. Those down the left side of the paper had names against all of them. On the right side there were not so many. 'Pete does the left side,' Bradey explained. 'See how this works?'

'Yes. He did a good job.' I read down the names, each of them had a time against them and either 'in' or 'out'. I recognized most of them, the hard-core customers who were in the place every night. But some were strange to me. And one of them was the mystery man they had mentioned the night before, the man who had come in just before the fight, meaning just after the rape.

He had a notation beside the X marking his spot. 'Tall, looked mean. No tip.'

I tapped the paper and showed it to Bradey. 'This is the guy we talked about last night. Remember anything more about him, Eric?'

He frowned and I went along the room and took down the chair he had been sitting in and put my foot up on it. 'He was here.'

He looked at me, thoughtfully, then went to his usual place at the beer tap. After a moment he began working his hands, miming the act of pouring beer and setting it aside for the waiters. Then he clicked his fingers. 'Yes. I remember. Was a guy around your size. Bit younger, maybe. Sat there watching the TV. Drank Coors.'

'Was he smoking?' The Murphy's Arms will burn down before Bradey lets it become a smoke-free environment.

'I'll have to ask Pete. He'll remember if he had to change the ashtray.'

'What colour hair?'

'Don't recall. Kind of a nothin' colour, you know. Not brown, not fair, somewhere in there.' He held up his hands. 'Hell, I wasn't that close to him. That's all I remember.'

I got up, replacing the chair on the table, and came back to him. 'That was really good, Eric. Tell me. Have you seen him in here before?'

He shook his head. 'Don't remember him.'

I checked down the list. 'Langdon and McWatters were over the other side of the room?'

'Yeah. They were the only two we knew for sure, Pete and me. We made a few guesses on the others but we want to talk to Chris before we mark anything in.'

'Do you have a copy machine?'

He nodded. 'Yeah, sure. Right over there. You want one?'

'Please. I'll leave this with you until Chris has put his names in. But there's a couple of guys I want to follow up on.'

He went into his office, an eight-by-eight room crowded with liquor crates. His desk had a copier next to it. He fed his list in and pressed the button. The copy rolled out and he handed it to me.

'Thanks a lot, Eric. This could give us the answer.'

'Hell of a thing, huh?' he said. 'Two murders. If we don't find the guy it could kill our summer business.'

'I'm doing my best.'

'You figure it was the same guy, both killings?'

'It looks that way. I'll know better after the autopsies. In the meantime, could you call when Chris comes in?'

'Will do,' he said and began lifting down the chairs from the tables.

Holland still wasn't at my office but he had sent me a fax to say he had been called into court. He would be down as soon as he could make it. Disappointing, but the news set me free to ring the men who had sat close to my Mr X in the bar.

He intrigued me. The time of his arrival made it possible that he was the rapist and the fact that he had vanished after the fight made it possible that he was also my killer. There was no evidence, but what the hell? I had nothing else to go on.

All five men who had been sitting near him were at work when I called. I got three no replies and two wives. From them I got the work phone numbers of their husbands. One of them was a truck driver, out on the road somewhere. The other one worked at the lumber yard just south of town. I got him on the phone and he had nothing for me. He'd been there with his buddy, watching the ball game, then the fight in the bar. The Jays had won, he told me. Great.

The phone rang as I hung up. It was Dr McQuaig. He would meet me at the funeral parlour right away to check the body.

I was there ahead of him and went back to the work-room where McKenney had taken the body. He was finishing up the cosmetics on another corpse, an old lady who probably hadn't worn lipstick for twenty years before today. He looked up. 'Dr McQuaig just phoned. He said he'd be here soon.'

83

'Good.' I stood and looked at McWatters's body. There was a lot less blood than there had been on Langdon. And I recalled that the interior of the truck had been stained, but not flooded, with blood, as the roadway had been when Langdon died. He hadn't suffered the same wound, I thought. Not that it made any difference to him. He was just as dead as Langdon.

McKenney finished his work and closed up the little tackle box that he used to keep the cosmetics in. He dusted his fingers daintily and looked at the old lady's face critically. 'You have to be so careful.'

'Right.' I owed him the courtesy, I'd be sunk without him, on days like this.

He stowed the make-up box in a cupboard and asked: 'You think the same man killed him as killed the American?'

'Seems logical but it's starting to look as if he did it a different way. This isn't the same kind of bloodstain.'

McKenney nodded. 'I noticed that when we brought him in. I'd say he was dying from that whack on the head and the knife wound caught him just before he died. That's why the blood didn't spurt everywhere.'

'What whack on the head? I didn't examine him.'

McKenney put his finger confidently on a spot behind the right ear. 'Feel that. The bone is pushed right in. He was hit with something heavy.'

I touched the spot and nodded. Yes, there was a crushed spot up in the hair, spongy to my touch.

'That's not all.' He pointed to a spot just under the breast pocket. 'See there, that's the knife wound. Right in under the heart. But you feel here.' He pressed on the spot. 'That's through the ribs.' His face creased into a mirthless smile. 'You can't tell me that was done in a fight. I'd say he was lying down and somebody went and stuck a knife in him, hit the rib and then wiggled the tip until it went through.'

'Never figured you for a Sherlock Holmes type,' I told him.

He sniffed. 'Death is my business. You see enough of it, you start to know things.'

There were voices outside the room and Dr McQuaig came in, carrying his bag. 'Les. Reid,' he nodded to both of us as he opened his bag and took out a pair of rubber gloves. He pulled them on and bent over the body.

First he did the same thing McKenney had done. He touched the stab wound, pressing on it. 'Hit a rib, had to adjust his thrust, I'd say. And had to lean on the knife pretty well, it went between the ribs.'

'Les thinks it was done while he was lying down.'

'That would make sense.' He stood up thoughtfully. 'With the attacker kneeling over him, no doubt. When he hit the rib he would just lay more weight on the knife handle.'

'Was he hit in the head first? That looks like a solid knock in the temple there.'

He stooped over the head injury, holding the sidepiece of his glasses as he peered at it. Then he fingered the wound, gently, probing. He didn't bother giving us the medical names of the bones that were pulverized. He just said: 'This could have killed him, if it didna' turn him into a cabbage. There was no need to stab him after that.'

I looked at McKenney who was soaking up every word. He shouldn't hear my next question. 'Les, I'm sorry to ask you, but it's a legal thing: I have to talk to the doctor in confidence. Could I ask you to let us have the room for a while, please.'

He didn't answer, just left the room without even looking at us.

'You've made the wee man mad,' McQuaig said.

'I had to try something out on you and if Les heard it I might as well put it in the paper.'

'True enough,' he said. 'What's on your mind?'

'I'm thinking we've got two murderers. Maybe McWatters killed the first guy. Then the second man killed him and tried to make it look like the same MO.'

He had the obvious question. 'Why would anyone do that?'

'They put this body in the lake. I wasn't supposed to find it. I think they wanted me to think that McWatters killed the hunter and went to ground.'

'That makes sense,' he said softly. 'Or maybe monkey see, monkey do. Someone who witnessed the first murder did the second.'

'If McWatters killed the first man he would have had his money on him. But he doesn't.'

'Maybe that's why he's dead,' McQuaig said. 'Somebody saw him rob the first chap, then killed him for the money he'd taken.'

'Great,' I said. 'But who killed him, that's what matters.'

There was a tall stool against one wall, all metal with a cold, round seat. McQuaig sat on it. 'It's a mystery, Reid. What are you planning to do?'

'There's a guy I want to track down. He was in the pub just after the rape last night. Then, after the fight, he was gone. I figure he must have seen the wad Langdon flashed, and followed him out and killed him.'

'Any idea who he is?'

'Not yet.'

McQuaig cleared his throat carefully. 'Reid. In case you didn't know, it's important you clear this one up very fast.'

'Dancy been on to you already?'

He nodded. 'Aye. He's ringing all the council members. He wants a meeting tonight to fire you and bring in the OPP.'

'How do you think the council will vote?'

'Well, you've got my vote, and Les McKenney's, I'd imagine. But there's the two Toronto yuppies, Palmer and Barnes. They're both full of theories about the economy and politics and crime. You know the way it goes. Don't be hard on the poor rapist, his daddy didna' tell him a bedtime story. I think you frighten them, Reid.'

'That gives me two votes out of five. Which means I

have until the meeting to find this sonofabitch, otherwise I'm looking for a job instead of looking for him.'

'I'll do what I can, Reid. I like the way you work and I've seen you get results time after time,' McQuaig said. 'I think Les an' I can talk the other guys around for a while, but the only way we can do it is to make this the test case, if you know what I mean.'

'Absolutely. Thanks for your efforts. I'm going to concentrate on the guy in the bar. I've got a feeling he did this as well as raping Amy Wilson. I'm hoping to get a lead on him very soon.'

'Let's hope you can,' he said and winked, picked up his bag and left. I went to the sink in the corner and washed my hands carefully, then went out to find McKenney. If his vote was important to my job, maybe I should be a little nicer to the guy.

I find apple-polishing hard work but I thanked McKenney for his help and went home for a moment or two of peace. Fred was out in the yard, pegging out laundry. She turned and lit up the yard with a beautiful smile. 'Hi, good lookin'.'

I gave her a hug. 'How are you holding up?'

'I'm fine. It wasn't me who was up all night. How are you?'

'Good. We've got a lead on a guy. I think he's the one who attacked Amy.'

Now she was serious. 'I hope you get him, Reid, she's like a zombie.'

'Still here?'

'Just until I've finished the laundry. Then I'm taking her down to her house so she can get her car and head for Toronto to stay with her parents until Doug gets back.'

'That would be best. Has she spoken to him?'

'Yes. She got in touch with his company and he called this morning. He's in Arkansas, won't be home until tomorrow morning.'

'And she's in the house?'

'Watching Lulu who's taking her nap. I told her she'd

be all right but she couldn't bear to leave her on her own.'
She looked at me soberly. 'That bastard screwed up her
life. It's going to take a while before she's back to normal.'

'You're going to have to warn all the women in your
play. Tell them to get a ride to and from rehearsals. If they
can't get one, have Carl or somebody drive them.'

She frowned. 'You think this guy is stalking the play?'

'I don't know what he's doing. It may be coincidence,
it may be that he was around the marquee last night and
saw all the women in the cast looking pretty and excited
and it got him fired up. All I know is I don't want any
reprise and if he's concentrating on the play I want to be
sure everyone's safe.' Especially you, I thought, but didn't
say it.

She finished pegging the clothes and picked up the
empty basket. 'Are you going to be there tonight?'

'Yes, for sure. But I'll be out of sight, keeping the place
under surveillance.'

'Good.' She reached up and gave me a brisk kiss. 'Got
time for coffee?'

'No. I have to be back at the office in case Holland gets
here, he's bringing a drawing kit to make a likeness of
this guy I want to talk to.'

She paused, the basket on her hip, right hand shading
her eyes, looking like the woman in an old painting my
grandmother had in her house when I was a kid. I kissed
her. 'Take care.'

'I can do better than that,' she said cheerfully. 'I can
run that computer of yours. Why don't I come in and set
it up for this investigation?'

The computer part didn't matter to me. With just myself
and a couple of volunteers working on the case it wouldn't
be hard to keep the details in my own head. But she would
be safer in the police station, and until I'd nailed the man
who raped Amy Wilson, her safety was my first priority.

'I would like that very much. Will you bring the baby?'

'Sure. She can play with all your lovely guns and things
while I tap away. I'll be there as soon as she's woken up.'

'You don't want to put her with the sitter?'

'Frankly, no,' she said. 'I like having her underfoot, she's a living doll. But if you think it'll give you a bad rep with the boys in the band . . .' She let it hang there until we both laughed.

'The heck with it. Bring her in, I'll lock up the firearms.'

By the time I got to the station there was a fax from Holland saying he would be there at three. Not as early as I had hoped, but his help was a gift, I couldn't complain. I sat for a moment, planning the way I would use him. Then I called all the businesses in town and told them to be on the lookout for anyone spending American money. Plenty of tourists do, of course, but I asked that they try to get an ID on the person who did it, the licence number of his car would be good, something that didn't make the guy suspicious. Everyone promised to do it and they all wanted to pump me about the killings but I pleaded pressure of work and kept the calls short.

The calls might pay off, but a man who had killed two people would know better than spend his loot in town. If he was a local guy he would sit on the cash for a while, then head down to Toronto maybe, or Montreal, somewhere he could change his money a few hundred at a time in a series of banks. He wouldn't spend up big in Murphy's Harbour. But it doesn't pay to overestimate the cleverness of criminals. They can be breathtakingly dumb.

Fred drove up to the station and I went out to help her, lifting the baby out of the car seat. Sam was right behind me and he pushed close to Louise, wagging his tail until she reached out and poked him with one finger.

'Mutual admiration society,' Fred said fondly. 'And I thought Sammy would be jealous of a baby.'

'You're talking as if he were just a dog.'

We went in, Fred carrying the car seat and the baby-bag she took everywhere. I flipped up the counter and she went through and set her bundles down beside the computer and reached out for Louise. I passed her over, happily. Babies and police work don't mix and I was hoping nobody saw me acting like a daddy when I was supposed to be the big hard copper.

Fred said, 'So refresh me. What am I setting up here?'

'I want a data bank, database, whatever, that keeps track of coincidences. If I interview somebody and he mentions a knife or a bicycle or a bloodstain or whatever, and then someone else comes up with another mention of the same thing, I want to have something better than my own memory to use in looking for it.'

Fred frowned, then set the baby down on the tiles and handed her a soft toy. 'That would need DB II,' she said. 'It also calls for some pretty good note-taking on your part. You can't just put down someone's name and address and expect the computer to sort out other coincidences.'

'I can keep the notes, but putting them into that thing would take me a lifetime. Can you transcribe stuff for me?'

'When Louise is good, yes. But she'll have to come first.'

'I understand, be glad of whatever you can do.' I wasn't going to argue, the computer program might crack the case for me. It was the way the British police finally tracked their 'Yorkshire Ripper'. A lot of police work consists of sifting data. Computers do it better than people.

The telephone rang and Fred answered, crisply. Then she frowned into it and when I looked at her questioningly she handed me the receiver without a word. She looked shaken so I was gruff: 'Chief of Police.'

The man's voice was a drawl. 'Well hi there, Chiefy. Was that the little woman I was just talking to?'

'What do you want?'

'I'm interested in that lady. Nice ass. Not overloaded in the tits department, but OK.'

'Who the hell are you?' I looked around at Fred. Her face was pinched up with a mix of shame and fear. I wanted to climb down the phone line and hammer the bastard at the other end.

'My name doesn't matter. We'll all get to know one another better as time goes on.'

I was wishing we had a tracer phone, one that displays the caller's number. I had asked for one in my last budget presentation but the council had turned me down. Now I was as powerless as any other victim of an obscene call. 'I know you already,' I said. 'You're a limp-dick little freak who gets off making dirty phone calls. When I catch up with you I'll wash your mouth out with soap.'

He sniggered. 'You've got me all wrong, Chiefy. I'm not a freak and I am certainly not a limp-dick. Just wait a while and your wife will know all about me.'

I lost it. 'You little scumbag, I'll snap you in half.'

He didn't laugh this time. But he sounded delighted. 'Listen, tough guy, it don't matter how tough you are. You're not the one I'm going to fuck.'

8

The word cracked in my head like a gunshot. I opened my mouth to speak but he had already hung up, laughing. Fred looked at me nervously. 'A phone freak, right?'

I reached out and held her shoulder. 'Yeah,' I said. 'Just what we need right now. I'm sorry you were here for it.'

'I'd have been answering the phone at home, just the same,' she said. 'Don't worry, dear. I had a creep like him phone me for months when I was living in Toronto. Finally had to change my number.'

I stooped and kissed her forehead. 'When I catch him I'll kick him right in the equipment.'

She smiled, tightly. 'From what I hear, his type's harmless.' Her face showed she didn't believe it any more than I did. Not after what had happened to Amy.

'That's what the textbook says but I'm going to leave Sam with you until I've found the bastard.'

Fred grinned but it was crooked. 'I don't think it's necessary, Reid, but if it'll make you feel better.'

'Lots.' I let go of her. 'Let's do it.'

'Yes, dear.' The strength had come back into her voice. 'Fear not, your womenfolk are safe as a church with Sam in our corner.' She smiled at me and it looked convincing, but then, she's an actress.

I clicked my fingers at Sam and he came to me at once, looking up into my face for the next command. Fred stood up as well, without arguing as she might have done before the phone call.

I touched her on the shoulder and told Sam: 'Go with

Fred.' He looked at me, then wagged his tail twice and went to stand in front of her.

'Good boy. Easy,' she told him and he sat down next to her chair, bonded to her until she set him free.

It was comforting to me but I asked: 'Have you still got that can of Mace I gave you?'

Now she tutted. 'Come on, Reid. Let's not get carried away.'

'OK. I'm sorry. I want you safe, that's all.'

'I'll be safe with Sam,' she said, fiddling with the computer, so she didn't have to look up. 'And I gave the Mace to Amy. She needed it, for comfort, if not for protection.'

'Good thinking,' I said. 'And I'm thinking if the caller saw you come here he must have been in town when you drove through. I'm going to ask around, see if anyone saw him making the call.'

'What about the computer?'

'This takes precedence.' I went out to the car, having to force myself to move slowly.

There is only one street telephone in town. It's in front of the government liquor store and I whisked up to it first. There was nobody around and the clerk in the store hadn't seen anyone making a call so I quickly hit the other places with phones. The restaurant, the grocery and both bars. Nobody at any of them had seen a man making a call.

That left me flat and I went back to the station, wondering if the caller was just the standard heavy-breather, someone with a quarter in his pocket, knowing enough about the way my station was run to realize that Freda answered the office phone. If that was so, he could have been calling from anywhere.

When I returned to the station, Fred was back to her bright, normal self. How much effort it was costing her I didn't know but there was no sign of anxiety and she didn't ask if I'd found the guy. All she said was: 'Talk to me about this program you want.'

'OK.' I sat down next to her and took out the list of names I'd been given at the Murphy's Arms. 'I'm going to talk to all these people, plus all the people who drove by the crime-scene last night, plus a whole bunch of others. What I need is to be able to check by computer to see if there are any connections.'

She frowned thoughtfully, then reached down to take the ball that the baby was holding up to her. 'Thank you, dear,' she said. She held it with one hand, still looking at me until Louise took the ball back and threw it clumsily, then got down on all fours and went after it.

I asked her: 'Will I need to use key phrases for you to search with? Or will you be able to trace connections by using any word in each file?'

'Any word at all,' she told me. 'It doesn't even have to be the name of something. I just set it up as a field and any word will trigger the connection.'

'Good. Then I'll head down to the pub and start getting some statements for you to work with.'

'I'll watch the phone here,' she said carefully. 'I'll have to head home around four though to feed Louise.'

'Just be sure to take Sam with you. I don't like the phone call, not after what happened last night.'

'Nor me,' she admitted. 'Do you want me to call the phone company? Ask them to put in one of those tracer phones in case he rings again.'

'Right. Tell them it's a police emergency. Otherwise they'll take a month.'

'Yes, boss.' She gave me a mock salute.

'And if our freaky friend calls back, make like you're whispering to someone this end, someone tracing the call. That'll get him off the line in a hurry.'

'I can handle that,' she nodded. 'Now I'll make a copy of this list and enter these names. Do you have that other list? The crime-scene people?'

I gave it to her and she went to the copier and ran both papers through it. She stood there, one hip jutting, unaware of the things it did to my libido and I thought for the thousandth time how dear she was to me. I would kill anybody who harmed her or the baby.

She handed the lists to me just as the phone rang. I reached for it but she shook her head and took the call. 'Murphy's Harbour Police.'

I waited, ready to grab the receiver but she was saying: 'The chief is out right now. He's already spoken to the TV and radio station and he tells me he won't be giving a news conference until he's completed some ongoing investigation.' She looked at me over the phone, mugging for approval at her cleverness. I gave her a thumbs up.

I waited while she disentangled herself from the reporter and when she was off the phone I said: 'I'll be at the Murphy's Arms. When Holland comes in, have him join me there, would you? And be careful, please.'

'Don't worry,' she said. 'That creep's not a threat. He's off playing with himself somewhere.'

There were only two customers in the Murph, but the bartenders, Pete and Chris were there. I figured they'd come in early to talk to me; there wasn't enough work for both of them. So I spoke to them first, rounding out my list of people who had been in the bar. Between them they knew most of the customers by name so that simplified things. But neither one of them could place the guy who had come in just ahead of the fight.

'Those two guys were in last night,' Mike said, nodding at the only customers in the place.

'In here all the goddamn time,' Chris confirmed. 'Always whinin' about not havin' a job. Never heard of either one of them looking for work.'

'OK. I'll talk to them,' I said, just as the door opened to admit Holland, carrying a briefcase. I excused myself and went to meet him.

'Thought I'd never goddamn get away,' he said. He was angry. Probably wishing he hadn't promised to come and help, now that he'd spent most of the day in court.

'Thanks for coming, Bill. I was just talking to the waiters. They saw a guy in here, just after the rape in town, just before the fight.'

'Doesn't mean a hell of a lot,' Holland said, and I could see he was going to need propping up for a while.

'The timing makes it interesting. He vanished after the fight. I figure he could be our man.'

'Could be a thirsty tourist, in for one beer.'

'Tourists tip. He didn't.'

Holland shook his head. 'Well, suit yourself. I've got the Identikit. Want me to work with them?'

'If you would. Come on, I'll introduce you.'

I led him down the room and went through the formalities, then asked: 'Can you guys spare a minute to work with Sergeant Holland? He wants to make a picture of the guy at that table.'

Holland opened his case and set out the Identikit and Chris grinned with pleasure. 'Hey. I seen one o' them on TV. Does it work?'

'Let's find out,' Holland said cheerfully. 'Now, what shape face did this guy have? Round, square, what?'

'Long, kind of square,' Chris said and Holland picked the proper component out of the set of choices and set to work.

I left them to it and went to talk to the two customers. The waiter's assessment was accurate. A sorrowful pair of losers from a place even smaller than Murphy's Harbour, lying north of us. I guessed they'd been in some kind of brawl in their own local bar and been banned. That's why they'd turned into regulars here. We were the nearest town.

Both of them had a good memory of the fight itself. Langdon had impressed them with his speed and toughness. He had taken the first punch which had knocked him off his chair but he had been on his feet, punching back before McWatters could deliver the traditional boot in the teeth. Aside from that they could remember nothing of value. Looking at their beer-softened faces I was not surprised.

They got a little sly, pumping me for details of the killings but I just beamed and asked them to call if they remembered anything else and went back to the bar where Holland was finishing up.

Chris, the waiter who had been working hardest with him was bobbing with excitement. 'That's him. That's the guy. That's just how he looked.'

Well, maybe he had, if he was a robot. An Identikit likeness is a little less than human. The lines and angles look like they came from a machine shop but it does give you something for people to compare with their lousy memories. Allowing for that, the stranger was a square-faced man in his thirties. He had medium-length hair and a closed expression that gave nothing away. He was clean-shaven and his face was neither fat nor thin. That would mean he was a medium build. 'How tall was he? Any idea?' I asked.

'Yeah. He'd be taller'n me by a couple inches.'

'Six foot,' Holland judged. 'And by the look of that face he'd go around one seventy-five.'

'Yeah. Not skinny. Not fat,' Pete nodded. 'Hey. Can we get a copy of that?'

'If you're sure it's a good likeness, yeah,' Holland said and carried the kit to the copier. We all watched the copy come off the machine. Holland checked it anxiously. 'Good. None of the pieces moved.' He reset the machine for ten copies and pressed start while Pete took the first one over to his boss.

Holland handed some of his copies to me. He was still gloomy. 'This is too easy, Reid. This could be just some guy in here having a beer. There's no connection between him and Langdon or the Indian.'

'None we know of yet. But this is where Langdon set himself up to be robbed. He flashed that big roll of bills, somebody wanted it. They followed him. He wouldn't hand it over and they knifed him.'

'All that makes sense,' Holland said. 'But you don't know it was this guy.'

He was right, but there's more to police work than logic. Luck plays a part, and instinct. One of the best cops I ever

97

worked with was no rocket scientist but he had a feeling about people and he was right more often than not. And now I had a feeling about this guy.

'He's worth finding.'

'So, where do we look?' He was sulking and it was starting to get on my nerves.

'Look, Bill. I appreciate your help, but if you want to quit, that's OK.'

He looked at me levelly for a long time, without speaking. Then he said, 'OK. I'm being a soreass. Where do we look?'

'In town first; I'll circulate these pictures after the guys in here have had a good look.'

'Right.' He slapped me on the arm, an apology for his short temper.

Eric Bradey was looking at the picture, his face creased up thoughtfully. He looked up at me, rapping the picture lightly with the backs of his fingers. 'I've seen him, not long ago, I know it, but I can't remember where.'

'Try thinking of places you didn't see him,' Holland said. 'Like it wasn't in church, was it?'

'For sure not,' Bradey snorted. 'Wasn't at the house. Wasn't outdoors. Must've been here.' He threw up his hands. 'I see everybody here. How'm I gonna remember?'

'You saw him but Chris and Pete didn't? Have I got that right?'

'Yeah. They saw him last night, not before.'

'So you weren't open when you saw him in here,' I suggested and he clapped his hands triumphantly.

'That's it. He was in here last week, just before we opened. He wanted to sell me a bearskin.'

The hair prickled on the back of my neck. 'Langdon was hunting bears. This guy must be the guide he hunted with.'

Bradey looked at the picture again and shook his head. 'The only bear guide I know is Willy Veale. This isn't Willy.'

I agreed. 'That's not Willy. He's an older man, in his sixties.'

One of the two customers called out: 'When the prayer meetin's over, can we get a couple beers here?'

Bradey handed me the picture and went back to his beer pumps, pulling two fast beers. Chris whisked away with them in that funny skating motion waiters use. Holland said: 'Let's go see this Veale guy.'

'Right,' I said. 'Thanks for the help, Eric. If this guy shows up in here, give me a call real fast. Otherwise, keep this quiet, OK?'

'OK, Reid. You think it's him?'

I shrugged and smiled helplessly and he nodded. I hoped he would be rushed off his feet with customers that day so he wouldn't have time for gossip.

Holland was happier now. As we walked out he said: 'I like this better. Maybe this guy met Langdon on the hunt. He saw Langdon's money and followed him down.'

'Maybe it's that simple. Let's go check Veale,' I said.

'OK,' Holland said. 'You got a cellular phone in your car?'

'No. Just a radio.'

'I'll bring my phone,' he said. 'In case we need to call in some troops.'

We drove out of town the northern way, over the bridge instead of past the police station, so I radioed Fred to bring her up to date. She reported that the major media were getting excited now there had been a second murder. A couple of reporters had come back again and some from the Toronto papers and radio stations. She had a bunch of them in the office.

'Things must be peaceful in Bosnia, they're stuck for news.'

'Could be. But worry not, I've mostly shooed them away – they're poking around town asking people how the news makes them feel.'

'Thanks for the tip, whatever you can do to keep them out of my hair is great.'

'Do my best. Where are you going now?'

'The press guys may be monitoring this frequency, so let's keep it secure, please. Remember I told you what the American was doing yesterday?'

'Right.' She spoke slowly, recalling, but did not blurt out her answer.

'I'm heading up there to talk to the guy in charge. Should be back in a couple of hours at the most.'

'Gotcha. Take care.' She hung up.

'We were lucky the media people didn't find us in the pub,' Holland said. 'That's all we need, a trail of reporters and TV cameramen tagging after us.'

'It's a problem sometimes, when I'm here on my own,' I told him. 'They stick to me like snot to an army blanket.'

Willy Veale's camp was hidden away down a logging road that cut in from another secondary road off the highway. It was bumpy, especially when I made the final turn on to the logging track.

I hadn't been out there since I first took this job and spent a week familiarizing myself, driving the whole area. But the cabin hadn't changed any, it was built from hand-squared logs and had a sign that looked like it had been painted when Veale came back from the Korean war. It stood up a sloping driveway and had a couple of smaller cabins around it, shabby and abandoned-looking now. I guessed Veale had intended to run a live-in camp at one time but hadn't had any takers.

'Desperate looking hole,' Holland said. 'Who in hell would stay here?'

'Nobody does. They come for the day and he guides them to a bear. He baits the bears and takes his hunters with him to knock them over while they're eating.'

'Real nice,' Holland said disgustedly. He opened his door to get out and at once a big ugly dog came roaring at him from the front of the cabin. He shut the door quickly and the dog jumped up at his window, a black and brown mass of hatred.

'What now?' Holland asked. 'You're the dog handler.'

100

'Not that one,' I said. 'Looks like his mother was a Rottweiler and his daddy was a Mack Truck.'

'The hell with his pedigree. What are we gonna do?' He had to raise his voice over the bellowing bark of the dog.

'Unless Veale is deaf, he'll come out and talk to us.'

We waited, ignoring the dog and the front door opened and a rangy stooped man came out. He had grey hair and he was smoking a cigarette. He said nothing, just watched his dog raise hell.

I wound my window down. 'Police!' I shouted, in the moment before his dog bounded around to my side and tried to take my head off.

The guy on the porch grinned broadly but did nothing to call off his dog. I tried one last trick, turning on the siren for a quick blast. His dog took that as a challenge and started tearing at my tyres.

'Screw this,' I said and backed down the driveway as fast as I could. The dog bounded beside us, barking and snapping. At the road I braked and drove up again. The dog was a little in front of the door, stretching to keep up. I goosed the accelerator and opened the door crisply, slamming him in the haunches. He rolled head over heels up the slope, bi-yiking like a puppy that's been stepped on.

Now I stopped the car and got out, my hand on my gun, ready to drop the dog if I had to. Veale had trained it to be mean. I could be meaner.

He flung his cigarette away and stormed down the slope towards me. 'What in hell you think you're doin'?'

'Giving your dog an obedience lesson. You got a licence for it?'

'Licence? I don't live in town, I don't need no licence.'

'Yes, you do.' From the corner of my eye I could see the dog sneaking away to its left, behind me. It was trained to hunt bears. It would treat me like one, biding its time until I was preoccupied, then savage me. I told Veale: 'Call it off or I'll shoot it.'

101

He had one eye that drooped and he turned it on me, his head tilted cunningly, doing nothing about the dog. I drew my gun and turned to face it. It was ten yards away, lying coiled on itself, ready to spring. I raised my gun and Veale roared: 'Kurt! Bed!' and the dog backed up and trotted to the porch.

'You had a hunter here yesterday. Name of Langdon, an American.'

Veale didn't answer at once. He was wearing a down-filled vest, the front blackened with grease. He dug into the pocket and pulled out a soft pack of tobacco and papers and began rolling himself a smoke. He looked at me with the same sly tilt of the head. 'So?'

I looked at the grease and remembered the rapist's glove I'd taken from Amy Wilson. It had the same greasy look. 'So somebody stuck a knife in him and took his money.'

He licked his cigarette paper and rolled it. 'Wasn't me.'

Holland had come up from the car with a copy of the likeness. He held it out. 'Who's this guy?'

Veale gave it a glance and then dropped his eyes, patting his pockets for a match. 'You tell me,' he said at last as he found a light and struck it.

'That's not how it works,' I said. 'This guy was selling bearskins in town. Does he work for you? What?'

'Don't look like nobody I know,' Veale said. He had both eyes half shut now, against the thin smoke of his little cigarette.

'Who's here with you?' Holland asked.

'Just my dog,' he said and coughed.

I turned to Holland. 'Call the motel and ask the Whelans who they saw here yesterday. Could you do that, please, Sergeant?'

'Right.' He recognized the game I was playing and walked back to the car where he took out his cellular phone and lounged against the door while he pretended to talk into it.

I leaned on Veale. 'OK, Willy. You've got about a

minute. Then I'm talking to the guys who were up here with Langdon yesterday when he got his bear.'

He didn't answer so I spelled it out for him. 'Either you talk to me or I find enough things wrong around here to have the Natural Resources' people revoke your licence.'

He gave a little smirk. 'You din't say you was talking about yesterday.'

'This guy' – I held up the picture – 'was he here yesterday?'

Now he reached out one hand and took the picture. 'Coulda been.'

'You can do better than that, Willy. Who is he?'

I turned to look at Holland, who was watching me as he talked on the phone. I flashed him a wink and he nodded into the phone as if answering the guy on the other end. Finally he flipped the phone shut and dropped it on the car seat. As he came up I told him: 'Willy's starting to remember things, like our friend was here yesterday.'

Holland took his cue. 'That's what I just heard. No name but they described him for me.'

Veale dropped his cigarette on a rock and put his foot on it. 'Was a guy here. Came up ahead of the other guys a couple minutes. I figured he was with them.'

Holland sneered at him. 'And you never asked. Instead of saying: "Where's the hundred bucks for going on the hunt?" you just took the whole buncha them out to your bait line and stood there while one of them shot a bear?'

Veale still tried to change the subject. 'Did it with a crossbow. One shot. Far as from here to that hemlock.'

I sighed. 'This isn't a game, Willy. This is for real. Let's have the truth or I charge you with accessory to murder and you go to jail for the rest of your sorry life. Those are the rules. Now, what's this guy's name?'

'Steve,' Veale said. 'Yeah. Steve. He told me that.'

'Don't bullshit me,' Holland thundered. 'This guy works for you. You pay him and all you know is his name's Steve?'

Veale looked at us out of the corner of one eye. 'I never said nothin' about him workin' for me.'

'I've heard enough of this,' I said. I took him by the wrist. 'Willy Veale,' I said. 'You are arrested on a charge of murder. You are not obliged to say anything.' That was as far as I had to go. He pulled his arm away and stiffened. 'Now just a goddamn minute. I never killed nobody.'

'You didn't have to do it yourself. You're hiding the guy who did. Give us his name and where he is now and I'll see what I can do about dropping the charges.' The voice of sweet reason.

Veale rubbed his face with his left hand, lowering his eyes. 'Awright,' he said. 'It's Stu Oliver, he's my sister's kid. Been workin' around for a month. Ever since he got out of jail.'

9

Holland looked like a sweepstakes winner, too excited to speak. I wasn't so sure. We still had nothing more than our suspicions to go on. Veale's news just made them look more accurate.

'Is he here?' I asked.

'No. Wen' into town last night in my truck. Said he'd likely be back today sometime.' Veale was nervous, sucking on his little roll-up cigarette as if it were an airhose. 'What's he s'posed to done?'

'What's the licence number of your truck?' I asked.

'I forget,' Veale said and Holland grabbed him by the front of his shirt. 'Number,' he hissed. 'Gimme the number or I'll tear your head off an' feed it to the goddamn dog.'

'Awright.' Veale dropped his smoke and put his boot on it. Holland eased up, letting go of him. 'It's JM 6000.'

'Make?' Holland snapped.

'A Chev, "S" truck, long body.'

Holland went to the car. I took over the questioning. 'Which town was he going to? Did he say? Parry Sound, Sudbury, Toronto?'

'He di'n say. I figured somewhere would take him couple hours, otherwise he'd've been back last night.'

'Was he out for a good time, business, what?'

Now he reached for his makin's again, his defence against direct questioning. 'He don' tell me much. He's a grown man.'

'How old?'

'Thirty-some.'

'What jail did he get out of?'

Veale concentrated on licking his cigarette paper, clutching the paper sack in the folded fingers of the hand that held the cigarette while he reached for a match with his other. 'Was in Millhaven,' he said.

Millhaven is maximum security. You don't get sent there for cheating on your income tax.

'What was he in for?'

Veale was going through the lighting-up ritual and he gave a noncommittal shrug. I slapped his hands down. He looked up to protest but thought better of it. 'Jesus. You guys is rough.'

'Quit screwing with us, Willy. What was he in for?'

He still hesitated, then before I could ask him again he spoke, choosing his words with great care. 'He hit some guy.'

'How hard? Did he kill him?'

He frowned, trying to work out a way of quantifying pain. 'He hit 'im. Like no, he didn't kill 'im.'

It couldn't have been far short of murder or he wouldn't have ended up in Millhaven. I began to feel a little of Holland's confidence. This guy had to be our killer.

Holland was standing by the car, using his cellular phone. He shouted to Veale. 'That's Stuart Robert Oliver, born November 19th 1963, right?'

'Yeah.' Veale said it slowly, stowing his tobacco bag in his vest pocket, watching me warily as he took out his matches again.

I let him light up, then said: 'Come on, Willy, let's take a look inside.'

'What for?'

'To see if Stuart Robert Oliver just happens to have snuck back while we were out here talking.'

'He's out. I told you. He's away in my truck.'

'OK, then let's make sure your truck's gone. Show me around.' I gave him a tap on the arm and he turned away and led me around to the back of the cabin. There were a couple of rickety log buildings out there. One of them was where his truck lived. Its earth floor was stained with oil and there were cans of oil on shelves and a forty-gallon gasoline drum with a hand-operated pump in it. But the space was empty now.

Next to it was another low building with no windows. I figured it was his icehouse but I checked it to see Oliver wasn't hiding there. He wasn't. It was bitter chill inside, filled with lake ice gathered through the winter and covered with sawdust. There was an oil drum with a lid on it standing in one corner. I checked the contents, a few plastic-wrapped packages, heavy and slippery.

'That's meat for the bears,' Veale said.

I closed the drum. 'OK, so let's see inside.' I motioned to the back door of his cabin.

He looked at me, narrowing his eyes against the smoke of his roll-up. 'You gotta search warrant?'

'Don't need one, you just invited me in,' I said and nudged him forward again. I wasn't about to go in first in case his bear-dog had a twin brother waiting in there to tear my leg off.

He swore softly and pushed in. There was no dog, but the stink of dead cigarettes made my stomach roll. An old enamel plate on the table was piled six inches high with butts.

I glanced at them, seeing that they were all the remains of his own thrifty little roll-ups. His nephew hadn't come marching home with money in his pockets for tailor-mades, although maybe he was smoking them now, courtesy of Thad Langdon's severance pay.

There wasn't much else to look at in the room. The cabin had no electricity, no running water, just a hand-pump in the cracked sink. And there was an honest-to-god icebox with a drainpipe running right out through the floor of the cabin.

Except for the pile of butts, the place was tidy. There was a coffee pot on the woodstove, which was burning, and one coffee mug and one plate upside down on the countertop beside the pump. His breakfast dishes, they

107

bore out his statement that Oliver had been away overnight.

There were two rooms off the kitchen. One had a double bed and an old pine chest of drawers. There were a couple of coats hanging on the wall and a gun rack with a rifle and a shotgun. Veale's room. The other had a single bed which had not been slept in but there was an Adidas sports bag lying on it. 'This belong to your nephew?'

'Yeah? Why?'

'I want to take a look at it.' I picked it up and brought it into the kitchen, dropping it on the table.

'Why you lookin' at his stuff?'

'Because's he's wanted for murder and this could help. Just watch, will you?' The way he was dragging his feet on every request was starting to read like jailhouse politics. I wondered if he'd ever been inside. It would explain his affinity for his nephew.

Holland came in, carrying his cellular phone as proudly as a lawyer in a fancy restaurant. 'They'll call when they find him,' he said. 'An' I've got some guys coming up to stake this place out.'

Veale drew the last quarter inch of value out of his smoke and added its corpse to the pile on the plate. 'You gonna tell me what you all think he done?'

Holland pulled out his own cigarettes and lit up happily. 'Sure thing. He knifed a coupla guys last night. One of them was that hunter you had up here yesterday. The other was an Indian from the reserve down at Murphy's Harbour.'

Veale looked at him for a long time before answering. 'That wasn't Stu,' he said softly.

'It wasn't?' Holland asked mockingly. 'That's not the way I hear it. I was just having his sheet read to me. He kicked one guy half to death. Beat some other one silly with a flat-iron.' He turned to explain to me. 'Let some gay pick him up in Toronto, then rolled him, beat him so bad the guy's brain-damaged. I'm telling you, he'd have used anything was there. This is one bad bastard an' we're gonna get him.'

108

'This is his stuff.' I flipped the Adidas bag. 'Let's check it.'

'You need a warrant,' Veale said, but there was no certainty in his voice.

'We're in hot pursuit of a criminal, to wit Stuart Robert Oliver. We can enter any premises and conduct searches as required,' Holland said roughly. 'So don't screw us around or you'll be inside for obstruction.'

He was lying, we were just two cops on a fishing trip but his confidence shut Veale up.

'You were just going to take the stuff out of the bag and show me, weren't you?' I said, and Veale looked at me oddly, then nodded. It was working. Good cop, bad cop. Holland could crack the whip, I would be in charge of the carrots.

Holland took the hint and said nothing while Veale lifted out the few things in the bag. Two work-shirts, socks, a pair of green work-pants, underwear. Even a toothbrush and a razor, wrapped in a threadbare towel.

'He could buy all of this at a Goodwill and have change out of a fifty-dollar bill,' Holland said. 'He's not coming back.'

'He's got my truck,' Veale said.

'And he's got his father's eyes and his mother's curly hair. And he ain't giving any of it back,' Holland said. 'You can kiss it goodbye, Willy. He'll steal a couple of plates for it and head off, south maybe, over the border.'

'Is he on parole?' I asked.

Veale shook his head. 'No. He done all his time.'

'Yeah,' Holland sneered. 'He was a hardass in jail. He didn't get any time off for good behaviour.'

'When did he get out?'

'Week ago. And he doesn't have to report to anyone, he's free and clear.' Holland puffed happily on his cigarette. I could see he'd marked the case closed. He could go home and start telling war stories.

'When did he get here, to your place?' I asked Veale.

'Three nights ago. I pick up my mail Tuesdays at the

post office in Honey Harbour. There was a letter sayin' he'd be on the highway that night so I waited.'

'Why'd he come to you?'

Veale sat down at the table. 'His mother's boyfriend won' have him around. Like last time Stu was out he punched the sonofabitch out. Like Stu ain't worried about him, but he won't go against his mom.'

'Sweet,' Holland said. 'Isn't that nice, Reid?'

'How long's he been bad?' I wanted a better profile of the man than I could get from the courtroom statistics Holland knew.

'A while,' Veale said calmly. 'Like he started out same as any kid, playin' hookey, takin' stuff. When he kep' it up they put 'im in reform school.'

He added his butt to the toppling pile on the plate and then, surprisingly, picked up the plate and emptied it into the stove. It seemed to me he was uncomfortable with what he knew.

'Did he have a bad time in reform school?'

Veale set the plate back on the table, placing it as carefully as if it were a game piece. 'Yeah,' he said at last. 'Yeah. Some of the big kids got at him.'

Holland was watching me, working out what I was after. He had the moxie to keep quiet while I kept on. 'Did that turn him on to guys?'

Veale shook his head, then went back to the stove, lifted the lid with the iron tool and spat into the flames. 'Made him mean.'

'That's understandable.' Reid Bennett, the voice of sweet reason. 'Did he talk to you much about it?'

Veale shook his head. 'Not much. Just the one time.'

Holland said, 'So he had a bad time. Makes your heart ache for him. OK. So enough history. Where was he going when he left?'

Veale shrugged. 'Into town he said, I told you.'

'To do what? Get drunk, pick up a girl, what?' I asked.

'He was dead set on gettin' laid when he lef' here. Said he was gonna get himself a nice juicy piece ass.'

110

'What kind of voice has he got, Willy?' I asked him. 'Does he talk rough, or like he worked in an office in the city?'

Veale snorted and I realized that he had real affection for his nephew. 'Got a voice could charm the pants off'f a china doll.'

The words chilled me. Given his history, Oliver was our rapist and he was still loose and he was stalking my wife. I kept the anxiety out of my voice. 'Quite a guy,' I said.

'Hell of a guy.' Veale began his tobacco ritual again. 'Anything bad he done was done to him first. People oughta think of that.'

Holland lost patience and collapsed the mood. 'Yeah, sure. Like somebody beat his brains out with a goddamn flat-iron. Right?'

I saw Veale's face close down like a store shutter. Damn Holland.

'If we get him, I'll make sure you get a chance to speak up for him in court,' I said but Veale's face didn't change. It was no good saying more so I signed to Holland to follow me and went outside.

'Oliver's the rapist,' I said when we were clear of the cabin.

'You sure?'

'Yeah. His description fits, and so does his MO. He raped the woman but didn't do anything more, the way most rapists do. And he was wearing gloves that smelled of grease, bear grease, I reckon.'

'Sounds like it could be, but you'll need more than that.'

'I'll get more. What worries me is that Fred got an anonymous phone call, a guy with a smooth voice, saying he was going to rape her.'

'Jesus Christ.' Holland went rigid. 'You better get back down there.'

'I've left Sam with her, he'll take care of her until I get back. But I want her to be on the lookout for Oliver. Can I use your phone?'

'Sure.' He handed it over and walked off a polite few paces while I dialled.

Fred answered with a French accent and I smiled. She was OK.

'Hi, love. It's Reid. Got some news.'

'Good news, I hope.'

'Yes. It looks like the guy we want is Stuart Robert Oliver. He answers the description of the rapist. Just out of jail. His description and the licence number of a truck should be on the OPP radio and fax by now.'

'Yes. It's here,' she said. 'What do you want me to do?'

'Call the Murphy's Arms. Bradey has an Identikit likeness. Ask him to fax it up to you so you'll recognize this guy on sight.'

Her voice took on an airy lightness, she was acting for me. 'Sure you're not overdoing the security thing, old love?'

'Maybe. But I'd appreciate your having the picture there.'

'All right. Where are you?'

'Up in the bush at Willy Veale's hunting lodge.'

'Like Mayerling is it? Where the Austrian archduke and his mistress died?'

'Think squalor. I'll tell you about it later. Anyway. Take extra care, and get the picture, please.'

'Anything for a quiet life. When will you be back?'

'Just waiting for reinforcements. Should be about an hour, I guess.'

'Fine. You've got quite a fan club of media people waiting for you. I've kept them out so far but they're getting restless, keep coming and going.'

I was glad to hear that there were people around her but said only: 'Thanks for taking care. See you soon as I can.'

She said goodbye and I shut off the phone and gave it back to Holland. He asked: 'Everything OK?'

'Yes, thanks. Seems to be.' I looked at the police car. 'Hold on, I'll stow the car around back, out of sight. In case Oliver drives up while we're here.'

'Right. I'll get out of sight.'

He walked to the other side of the cabin and I drove around and turned, facing out ready to roll in a hurry if needed. Holland joined me and I asked about the help he had coming.

'Doing it by the book,' he said carefully. 'I've got three guys coming.'

'Didn't think you could spare three guys.'

He sniffed and looked awkward. 'Like, I called out the ERT.'

The Emergency Response Team. The SWAT team, to TV viewers. He was feeling a little foolish now but I didn't push him. They would take over, and they would stake this place out until Oliver came back or they were called off. 'Good.' I left it at that.

We went back into the cabin and Holland and Veale sat and smoked until I'd had enough and took a walk out around the property, getting the lay of the land.

I found the skin of Langdon's bear nailed to the back of the garage, the side that caught the sunlight. It was scraped down, drying well. Langdon had been right, it was a good-sized bear.

The Emergency team arrived about half an hour later. They were driving their big truck, filled with surveillance gear and weapons. Three fit young men, all with identical military moustaches.

They didn't pay much attention to me, just discussed the job with Holland. That made sense, he was their department, I wasn't. Looking at them I was reminded of myself and the guys in my platoon, twenty years before, in Nam, before the NVA and Viet Cong showed us what we were there for.

'I want the guy alive,' I said at last, when Holland had given his own instructions.

'That's up to him,' their leader said. 'He can give up or not.'

'He isn't carrying a gun, as far as we know. Don't drop him unless you have to.'

'Sure,' the leader said dismissively and turned away.

I shrugged and went back inside. Veale was still smoking, ignoring the activity of the ERT guys. He hadn't even switched on his little radio. 'I want to thank you for your help, Willy. If you hear from him, advise him to come on in. It'll be better for him. Or if you learn anything that will help us find him, give me a call, OK?' I don't carry business cards like city detectives do, but I wrote out the phone number for him and he looked at it and nodded.

'He ain' gonna give himself up. Not if he stabbed them guys.'

I shrugged. 'I don't think he did it. But it looks bad until he's cleared himself, can you tell him that?'

He nodded, not even looking up and I went out back to collect my car. When I drove out front with it, Holland was talking to his guys and they were clustered around him, professionally grim.

After a minute or two, Holland wrapped up and they all nodded and dispersed, carrying their M-16s. I wondered idly how they would set up their surveillance. I'd have put men forward, down the track about fifty metres so they could box Oliver in if he spotted them and tried to reverse out. Maybe they would. They had probably taken a cut-down version of the same infantry training I'd had.

They made Holland happy at any rate. 'If he tangles with those guys, he's history,' he said as we drove off.

'For sure,' I said, sounding as if I meant it.

Fred had been right about the media. There were half a dozen vehicles waiting outside the police station, radio and television station vans from as far away as Toronto. The reporters and camera people were chatting and drinking coffee but they swarmed the car when we got there, firing off questions before I had even opened the door.

'Ladies and gentlemen.' I held up my hand and got out. 'I'd appreciate your help, please. I have something for you to show on the air.'

The questions kept on flying while Holland got out, bringing with him the likeness of Oliver and holding it up. 'We're looking for this man who was in town here at

Murphy's Harbour last night. His name is Stuart Oliver.'
I chimed off his age and height and weight and they all scribbled and rolled their cameras.

'Why are you looking for him?'

'Did he kill both the victims?'

'What about the rape that took place last night?'

Those were the intelligent questions. There were dozens of others. I just said: 'We think this man, Stuart Oliver, can help us in our investigation. And by "us", I mean the local department and some volunteer OPP helpers, including Detective Sergeant Holland who made this Identikit likeness.'

That did what I hoped, it split the questioners into two groups. One went after him, but others kept on at me. Jean Norman, the TV reporter from the local station, was the toughest. 'Is the rape connected to the two killings that have happened here in the last twenty-four hours?'

'That's a possibility but I don't want to make any statements until our investigation has gone a lot further.'

There were a couple more rape questions but the one that floored me came from a radio reporter from CBC, our national network. 'It's reported that you've been fired. Why are you still working?'

She was one of those earnest young women without make-up who look as if they hate all military and police personnel as a matter of faith. I gave her a great big smile and said: 'Because I haven't heard the same erroneous reports that you have.'

Her voice went up most of an octave. 'This was from the reeve of Murphy's Harbour.'

'Well, if you're right, I'm sure he will tell me at some time. And now, if you'll excuse me, I have work to do.'

I gave her another big smile and went on by into the station. It didn't stop her, or the others, from following me but I went right on through the counter where it wasn't public.

The baby was asleep in her car seat with Sam lying beside her on the floor and Fred was sitting at the computer, keying something in. She did a little stage business of holding up phone slips for me and watching as I read them while the six or seven newshounds clamoured at the desk.

The messages were phonies. The top one read: *No news. I've faxed the likeness on to the bank and asked Millie to pass it around the stores in town. OK?*

The second said: *Nice work tracing this guy. Did he do it?* and the third one: *The American victim's brother was in. He's gone to the Murphy's Arms and wants you to know he's there.*

I bent closer to whisper confidentially: 'Thanks, love. You're brilliant. Have you got to leave soon?'

'When small fry comes to I'll have to take her home to feed her and that's it for the day; I have to get on with the plans for dress tonight. What's happening with you?'

'I should go and talk to Langdon.'

'Good luck, getting rid of this crowd.'

I straightened up and went to the desk. 'I don't have anything further for you at this time, folks. But I do have work to do and it's not going to be possible with you all in here.'

'You can't order us out,' the snappy young woman said. 'This is public property.'

'I'm not ordering, I'm requesting you as responsible citizens to stop hampering the work of this department. Would you all be kind enough to leave, please? As soon as I have developments to report I will set up a proper press briefing.'

They could have ignored me and stayed but their editors or whatever needed material and they had enough to keep them happy for an hour or two so they packed up slowly and left. One of the TV people called out to Fred: 'Aren't you Clarissa in that coffee commercial?'

'Only for thirty seconds at a time,' Fred told him.

He wanted to talk that up and asked her to pose with a coffee cup as she did in the commercials but she only smiled and said nothing and eventually he too gave up and left.

'Alone at last,' Fred said and I gave her arm a quick squeeze.

'Thanks for the notes. I think we're on to something with this Oliver character. He may or may not have killed those guys but he sounds like the man who attacked Amy.'

'You said "sounds".' She was nervous. 'Do you have any idea what Oliver's voice sounds like?'

'He sounds "smooth" was what his uncle said.' I took her arm. 'Be really careful, love. I won't be happy until he's inside.'

'Nor will I, to be honest,' she said, then brightened. 'But I'm sure you'll find him soon.'

'Sooner than that,' I promised. 'These media people can help us do it.'

'Speaking of which, I don't hear any cars driving away. Are they having a conference of their own?'

'No, Bill Holland's out there.' We went through to the window and looked out. Holland was holding court for them, flashing his Identikit picture. The cameras and microphones were all fixed on him.

'He's having a good time,' Fred said. 'Everyone wants to be famous.'

'Fifteen minutes each, right? Isn't that what you said?'

'Not me, dear, Andy Warhol.'

'Whoever. I'm off to the Murphy's Arms.'

'Have you eaten since breakfast?'

'Didn't think of it.'

'Men,' she said, and kissed me.

You had to hand it to Holland, he was keeping them spellbound out there. I was able to drive away without anybody following me, although I knew they'd find me soon enough when they chose to.

There were a dozen or more cars at the Murphy's Arms and Langdon's Cherokee was one of them. He had a gun rack in the back window, I noticed, but it was empty right now.

I walked in and found him at the bar, talking to Chris, the waiter. They looked up but Langdon ignored me and kept talking. Chris appealed for help with his eyes and I went to them.

'This here is Mr Langdon, he's the brother of the guy who was in the fight last night,' Chris said, passing him over like a relay baton.

I said: 'We've met,' but Chris had grabbed the opportunity and was gone to serve one of his tables.

Langdon said, 'What have you found out?'

'Got a lead on a guy who looks like he did it.'

'What's his name?'

'It's Oliver, Stuart Oliver. He's just out of jail.'

'What's he look like?' Langdon was holding himself erect, like a soldier, but his eyes were red-rimmed with fatigue. He was angry and dangerous, a grenade with the pin pulled. I wanted him out of circulation.

'They've got a picture at the bar. But he's not around. He's taken off in his uncle's truck.'

'Lemme see the picture.' He shouted it to Bradey who was standing at his beer pump. Bradey looked at me, then pulled out the picture and held it up for Langdon to see.

'Thanks,' Langdon said icily.

'He's not in town,' I repeated. 'But he's driving a truck, you could help me look for that.'

'You don' wan' me around, that it?'

'Do you want to help or not?'

He looked at me for a long moment before nodding. 'Yeah. Sure.'

'It's a red Chevy "S" truck, that's the compact. Easy plate to remember. JM 6000.'

'Where's he gone?'

'If I knew I'd be there, arresting him. I have to find that truck and I'm on my own.'

'Got a phone number where I can reach you?'

I gave it to him and he left, not looking back. Bradey left his taps and came over. 'Reid, something I wanted to tell you.' I waited and he said, 'I was thinking. You know, about that girl in the play gettin' raped.'

'You heard something?'

'Chris did.'

On cue, Chris came back to the bar and slid his tray on to it, unloading the dirty glasses. 'Yeah. Couple of guys were in, friends of Doug Wilson. You know 'em, Steve Amery an' some buddy of his from Honey Harbour. I heard 'em talking about what happened and one of them, Amery, he goes, yeah, I know who done that. I heard Roy one time sayin' that dummy at the marina was lookin' funny at Amy. An' it's right there next to where they were practising their play. He'd've been watchin' her act.'

'Jesus Christ,' Bradey said. 'That's young Yeats, Arnold's boy. He's strong as a horse. You should see him liftin' boats around up there.'

'Where are these guys?'

'They left, just when that 'merican came in askin' about his brother.'

'Thanks, Chris. I'd better get up there.'

I didn't run but I got out to the car and up to the marina in a hurry. We're a law-abiding town, but rape is a crime that brings out the vigilante in all of us. And a couple of guys with a bellyful of beer could make trouble.

The marina is next to the Lakeside Tavern on Main Street, on beyond the marquee, surrounded by its chain-link fence, its tall boat-storage racks mostly empty now, the cruisers they had contained all dispersed for their summer use. But the racks, and the few boats standing around the yard, made it hard to see what was happening inside.

I drove in through the gate and looked around. There was nobody about, even the gas pumps at the end of the dock were unattended. And it was quiet. All I could hear was the distant roar of an outboard motor up the waterway.

I debated giving a squeal on the siren but killed the idea. It would bring the goddamn newshounds down on me like a plague of locusts. So I took a quick walk around, looking for Jackie Yeats. He's the son of the new owners who took over when Walter Puckrin died. He'd be twenty-five, five-ten and muscular, normal-looking except for a wildness in his eyes. He doesn't talk a lot, one of those people we used to say were 'simple' but now have to call 'developmentally challenged'.

There was no sign of him and that was unusual. He was like a lizard for the sun and would always be out sitting on a boat hull if there was nothing to do.

There's a few buildings on the property, mostly down at dockside, where the attendant can get out to the fuel pump when he needs to. But there's a paint shop out in the middle of the yard and I saw that its door was shut. I went over and tried the door and it swung open.

There were two men there with Jackie. One of them holding Jackie's arms from behind. The other was about to drive his fist into the kid's gut.

I lost it. All my anger and frustration at the rape of Amy Wilson and the threat to Fred boiled over. I took two quick steps across the room and slammed a solid right hand into the guy's ear. He went down as if he'd been shot and I made a half turn and punched again, over Jackie's shoulder, right into the nose of the man holding him. It burst like a tomato, spouting blood.

He fell backwards and Jackie collapsed, his hands clenched around his groin.

The guy with the busted nose was conscious. He backed up on his heels, scrabbling away like a crab. 'On your feet,' I ordered and bent over the boy.

'It's OK, Jackie. We'll get you to the doctor's.'

He just moaned and lay there with his eyes closed. The guy who'd been holding him was standing up, groping in his pocket for a handkerchief. 'Pick up your buddy and bring him to the car.' I ran out and down to the repair shop. Arnie Yeats was in there, with a mask over his face, grinding down the hull of a cruiser.

He switched the tool off and flipped his mask down. It left a white circle around his mouth against the rusty red of his face.

He saw my anger. 'Jesus, Reid. What's up?'

'A couple of heroes have beaten Jackie up. I'm taking

them in. He needs a doctor, hospital would be better. I think they kicked him in the testicles.'

'I'll kill the bastards.' He ran out of the shop and I had to run after him. I got to him before the men came out of the paint shop.

'Don't touch them. They're under arrest,' I told him. And then he saw them and their damaged faces.

He turned and looked at me. 'Thanks, Reid,' he said softly. 'I'll take care of Jackie.'

The second one had come around by now and he staggered to the cruiser under his own power. I jammed the pair of them into the cage and drove them to the station, praying that the media would be gone.

All but one of them had. She was the bloody-minded radio woman and she came out of her car on the dead run, gabbling into her tape recorder. 'Are these men suspects in the murder case?' I ignored her, shepherding them out of the car and through the back door of the station. She tugged at the guy with the broken nose. 'How did you get hurt? Did the police officer hit you?'

He looked at her, over the bloody handkerchief he was clutching to his face. It was the moment when my tenuous hold on my job was at its weakest.

'Come on!' she yelled at him. 'Did he hit you? The people have a right to know.'

He checked in his tracks to speak to her. I was in his hands at that moment. Then he lowered his hands from his nose and hissed, 'Piss off.' I hid my smile and ushered him through the door.

She tried to follow us but I shut the door in her face and let her pound on it while I sat both men down at the desk.

The door from the station opened and Holland came out. 'What happened to these assholes?' he asked cheerfully.

'Assault bodily harm on the retarded boy at the marina.' My fist was hurting badly and I opened and closed the hand a couple of times.

121

'You're lookin' at six years,' Holland told them. 'How's that make you feel?'

The one who'd been punching the kid said: 'He raped Doug's wife.'

'What's your name?' I demanded.

'Steve Amery, Chief. You know me.'

'Your name?' I asked the other one.

'Don Ellis.'

'OK, listen carefully. Steve Amery and Don Ellis, you are under arrest.' I read them the whole song and dance and when I'd finished Amery started to snuffle.

'Oh fer Crissakes.' Ellis looked at him in disgust. 'Smarten up.' He was going to say more, acknowledging guilt, but the formal caution I'd read him had done its job and he said instead, 'Can I call my house?'

'What's the number?' Holland had his handy-dandy cellular phone and he dialled as Ellis dictated, then handed over the phone. I had Amery turn out his pockets, itemized his belongings and put them into an envelope which I sealed. Then I shepherded him into a cell, taking his belt and the laces from his work-boots. Steel-toed, I noticed. If he had kicked young Yeats the boy might die.

I studied his ear. It was swollen to twice its size and was split open in a couple of places. He needed a doctor. 'I'll call Dr McQuaig in to see your ear,' I told him. 'You sit there, wouldn't hurt to splash some cold water on the ear, keep the swelling down.'

'I'm going to sue,' he mumbled. 'P'lice brutality. I'm gonna talk to that woman outside, soon's I'm out of here.'

'Your privilege,' I told him. 'In the cell. You'll be safer in here where Mr Yeats can't find you and kick you like you kicked his son.'

That made him shut his mouth with a snap. I locked the door and waited until Ellis had finished his call. He folded the phone and handed it back to Holland. 'Do you have a lawyer coming?'

He ignored me, then turned out his pockets and let me seal his belongings away. Then he slipped out his belt

122

without being asked, kicked off his running shoes and went into the cell next to Amery's. I locked him in. His running shoes stank so I took a plastic bag from the bottom drawer of the desk and dropped them in, screwing the top of the bag tight and putting it back under the desk. Then Holland and I went through to the front of the station.

The radio woman was still there. She was haranguing Fred who had slipped into what she calls her 'Mrs Rich-bitch' voice and was giving her back as good as she got.

When she saw me the reporter called out: 'Officer! Why were those men arrested?'

That was a fair question so I told her. 'They're charged with assault causing bodily harm.'

'And who was the victim?'

'That isn't information you need at this time. If it becomes important for the public to know I will inform you.'

She turned to Holland. 'Sergeant Holland. You're a more reasonable man. The people have a right to know what's going on. Who did these men assault?'

Holland was still basking in the warmth of his fifteen minutes of fame and he said: 'Now, Ms — what's your name?'

'Collins,' she said impatiently.

'Ms Collins. You'll appreciate that we have a responsibility to guard the privacy of an injured person.'

'Was this a sexual assault?'

He started to answer this one for me when the phone rang. Fred picked it up, first ring and answered crisply. Then she said: 'Yes, he's here,' and handed me the phone.

'Hah,' the voice said. I'm so far removed from my days among southerners that I didn't realize for a moment it was a greeting, read 'hi'.

'Hello,' I said.

'Hah, this is Walter Langdon. Thought you might like to know I've found your missing truck for you.'

10

The reporter was watching me like a mongoose. I lowered my voice and asked Langdon where he was.

'I'm on the goddamn highway, that's where, at the Shell gas station a half mile up from your side road. The truck's right here.'

'Thank you. I'll join you there. Don't touch anything.'

The reporter had broken off in mid-sentence and was ready to fall into lockstep with me. I reached for a sheet of memo paper and scribbled: *Gone to the Shell station north of town. Truck there. Ask Bill to join me.*

I passed it to Fred who glanced at it. Then I told her: 'Could you call the doctor to look at the prisoners, please? Also, arrange a bail hearing.'

'Right away,' Fred said. She flipped the rolidex and picked up the phone.

The reporter rose to the bait. 'How badly hurt are those men? Who hurt them. Was it you, Officer?'

I looked at her and went out through the back door without speaking. The two prisoners were sitting on their bunks. Ellis's nose had stopped bleeding and he was rinsing the blood out of his handkerchief. It was almost clean. Amery was hunched over, one hand cupped over his bruised ear. I rubbed my aching knuckles and regretted hitting him.

The reporter's voice was still sawing the air behind me so I left through the side door and was into my car and away within seconds. I drove past the scene of the Langdon killing where a couple of old sedans were parked on the shoulder. Two farmers in green work-clothes were standing, hands in pockets, examining the bloodstain as if they intended to put in a bid on it. Thad Langdon had enriched their lives for them.

The gas station stood on an acre of land that had been chopped out of the bush. The pumps, office and coffee shop were all in the centre. There were haulage trailers and cars parked around the edge of the lot. Langdon was standing behind a trailer and he raised one hand when he saw me. I pulled in next to him and he led me down to the back of the trailer and pointed.

The pickup was sticking out of the trees where someone had made a clumsy attempt to hide it. Langdon bent and peered into the side window. He turned and straightened up as I reached him. 'Pretty damn hard to find,' he said sarcastically. 'Hell, it must've took me ten minutes.'

'Nice work. Thank you. The OPP patrol only comes by here about twice a shift, they could have missed it for a week.'

I hooked the tip of one finger under the door catch and tried it. It was locked, and so was the other side. Peering in, I could see a clutter of junk on the passenger side, a plastic pail with a lid, a pair of jumper cables, an axe head, the kind of oddments you would find in any countryman's truck.

Langdon had the obvious question. 'So I've found it, now what?'

'Now we check to see if anybody saw him.'

'That's it?' Langdon exploded. 'That's all we can do?'

'Maybe he's in having a coffee.' I walked over to the diner.

Behind me Langdon called: 'Don't waste your time. He ain't there.'

He wasn't. And the mom and pop who ran the place hadn't seen anyone leave the truck there. Pop, who pumped the gas, hadn't even noticed the truck. I showed them the copy of Oliver's picture and asked them to call if they saw him.

Langdon was pacing angrily. 'Not there, right?'

'It's one possibility eliminated,' I told him. 'When I get back to the station I'll get the media to circulate this location, see if anyone saw the truck being parked here.'

'So what now?' He was jumping with tension.

'We eliminate the next possibility, check that he's not lying out in the bush here with a knife in him.'

Langdon shook his head in disbelief but he plunged one way into the bush and I went the other, casting back and forth, covering a fan-shaped area out from the parked truck all the way down to the river that ran a hundred or so yards behind the station. I missed Sam's efficiency, he could have done it better than both of us together, and faster. But he was better employed guarding Fred and the baby.

When I came back to the truck, ten minutes later, Holland was there, talking to Langdon. 'Find anything?'

'No. He's not around.'

'Now what?' Holland asked.

'I've got a slimjim in the car.' I went and brought out my burglar tool and slipped it down between the glass and the outside of the door. Five seconds later I'd opened the door.

Langdon was looking at me with new respect. 'I figured you'd have to get a court order.'

'Don't talk this up, OK?'

I got a couple of plastic evidence bags and slipped them over my hands before touching anything, then went to work.

It was a long shot that there would be anything useful inside, but the first thing I saw, lying between the plastic pail and the transmission hump, was a work-glove, blackened with grease. It was a left-hand glove. The one left at Wilsons had been right-hand. I picked it up and sniffed. It had a rancid smell. It was all the evidence I needed that Oliver had raped Amy Wilson.

'What're you smelling it for?' Langdon wanted to know

'A glove like this was left behind after an attack that happened while your brother was still alive.'

Holland looked at it. 'You sure this is a match?'

'Positive. Let me bag it and mark it.'

They watched while I sealed the glove in its own plastic bag and marked it with the date and time.

Langdon watched in silence, then he asked: 'You sayin' some broad was raped last night?'

'Yes,' I said shortly. 'I think Oliver did it and then went on and killed your brother.' I put the gloves into my car and went on searching the truck. The pail was full of rusty tools, wrenches, a hacksaw and an old ball-peen hammer with the handle repaired with electrical tape. It could have been the instrument used to knock Jack McWatters on the head. I checked it carefully but couldn't see any blood or hair on it.

There was nothing but a few discount gasoline coupons in the glovebox. But behind the seat I found a flat plastic pint bottle of Seagram's '83, almost empty. I opened it and sniffed to make sure it was whisky then put the bottle into another evidence bag.

'One thing doesn't add up,' I said. 'The woman he raped noticed that the gloves smelled bad, but she didn't mention anything about liquor on his breath.'

'Meaning?' Holland wrinkled his forehead.

'Meaning there may have been two guys in this truck. One did the drinking, the other did the rape.'

'Maybe he held off the booze until after he'd banged her,' Holland tried.

'For sure he'd have been drinking first. The liquor store closes at six. The rape didn't happen until around eleven. I think Dave Stinson should fingerprint this, see if he gets anybody else's prints besides Oliver's.'

'How about checking at the liquor store?'

'I'll do that,' I said. 'But what I'm wondering is whether his uncle came into town with him.'

'I didn't think that sonofabitch was levelling with us,' Holland said grimly. 'But he won't be going anywhere.

Not with the ERT guys up at his place. We can talk to him later.'

Langdon spoke, in a low, angry voice. 'You both talkin' about stuff that don' matter to me. Where's this Oliver at? That's what matters.'

'He could be anywhere,' Holland exploded. 'We won't know till we find him, will we?'

'You asked me to find his goddamn truck an' I found it!' Langdon shouted back. 'An' now you stand around talkin' about other guys, other stuff. What about Thad?'

Diplomacy time. 'I'm sorry. And I'm grateful for your help in finding the truck. But a case like this isn't a hundred-metre dash. It's a marathon. You've brought us forward a mile but there's another twenty-some to go.'

He didn't answer, just turned away and stood there and I realized he was weeping. I gave Holland the nod to follow me and backed him out of earshot.

'Let's send him up to Stinson with the bottle, also the tool box. I want them checked to see if there's any of Jack McWatters's hair on them. He was clubbed with something.'

'Fine. But why send this guy?'

'It'll keep him out of harm's way and it saves one of us from going.'

'Fair enough. You got a seal for the bag?'

'Yeah, and for the tools.' I went to the car and dug into the plywood case I had made to contain my evidence kit. I sealed the bag containing the whisky bottle and wrote the date and time and signed it. Holland did the same and I bagged the pail of tools and we waited until Langdon turned around, composed.

'I was wondering if you would do me another favour?'

'Find this Oliver? Sure thing.'

'Maybe not in one swoop, but it'll help. Could you deliver this evidence to the crime-scene officer at Parry Sound?'

'How far's that?'

I told him and he said: 'Sure. That it?'

I handed him the bags containing the tools and the whisky bottle, and told him how to find the police station. He gave me a mock salute and left. We watched him go and then Holland asked: 'Are you going to check with the liquor store?'

I yawned, realizing suddenly how deeply tired I was. Holland shook his head. 'Listen. I'll do it. You go catch a couple hours' zuzz.'

'I'm going to have to.' I rubbed my eyes. 'I have to be bright-eyed and bushy-tailed tonight in case the guy tries another rape. And that means I have to collapse for an hour.'

'Go to.' He made a little shooing gesture.

'Oh. Hell.' I remembered Amery and Ellis. 'I've got to get a bail hearing going for those two guys who assaulted the kid.'

'I'll join you down there,' he said. 'I'll check the liquor store first.'

I whisked down the highway and pulled into the lot as Dr McQuaig was leaving. He stopped his car level with mine to talk.

'I've checked them. The one chap's nose is all right. He's had it broken before, it's just swollen. But the other one's ear may stay like it is. An old-fashioned cauliflower ear.'

'I shouldn't have hit him.'

'You should have pulverized him,' he said angrily. 'I was at the hospital when they brought young Jackie Yeats in. It's touch and go if they'll save his testicles.'

'Thanks for coming down, Doc. This is getting bloody.'

'I've dressed his ear and done what I can to reduce the swelling. He shouldna stay in jail though. If he gets to the hospital they may put leeches on it, that would help.'

I frowned at the thought but he didn't expand so I told him. 'The magistrate's coming soon. He'll let them go.'

'Fine. But if you need support in court, call me. I canna countenance what they did to that poor boy.' He nodded briskly and got back in his car.

I watched him drive away and then went inside. Fred

was playing with the baby while she talked on the phone. She flashed me a smile but I could see she was getting anxious. 'He just walked in,' she said and handed me the phone. 'It's the magistrate for the bail hearing.'

I took the phone and fixed the bail hearing while Fred collected all of Louise's things and put them into her bag. By the time I got off the line she was ready to go.

She stopped and handed me a written note. 'This was a call from a Rick Harding at the forensics department in Toronto. Said he used to work with you.'

'Yes, we were in Toronto together, fifty-two division. What did he want?'

'Said the autopsy is going to take place tomorrow, but said to tell you that the deceased' – she paused and laughed – 'honestly, he said, the deceased.'

'He always was a stickler for detail. What about this deceased. He was a cross-dresser, what?'

She laughed again. 'Much more butch. Said he had a sheath hanging down his back, said it would fit a Tennessee toothpick.'

'That's a long, thin-bladed knife, like the one that was used to kill him and McWatters.' I filed the information away. Maybe McWatters had come after him for round two of their fight. Maybe Langdon had tried to hold him off but McWatters had taken the knife off him, he was quick and tough enough to do it. And then what? I gave up the effort of trying to work it out. I needed that sleep.

Fred was concentrating on the baby now. 'I have to take her home and feed her,' she said when I hung up. 'And I'll keep her with me tonight at the rehearsal.'

The baby smiled and Fred gave her a hug. 'I can't leave her with a sitter.'

'I have to work. I have to try and find out who attacked Amy.'

'Don't worry about us,' she said. 'I'll take Lulu with me to rehearsal and Sam will be there to take care of us.'

'I'll be there as well.'

'You look beat,' she said anxiously. 'Can't you take a break?'

'After the bail hearing I'll grab a couple of hours. I want to come to the rehearsal, talk to your people about last night. See if anybody saw anything.'

'Right.' She was carrying the baby and she picked up the car seat with her left hand. 'I'll get on home.'

'Let me.' I took the car seat from her. The phone rang but I ignored it. 'I'll get you into the car.'

'I'll manage,' she said gently. 'Answer the phone. I'll see you at home, soon.'

There was nothing to say. I gave her a squeeze and she left, with Sam at her heel.

The caller was Dave Stinson. He sounded cheerful. 'Well, I got through the whole day without going out on uniform patrol.'

'Anything else is a bonus. What did you find out?'

'Your American got here with the bottle and the tool box. The tools will take some time, but I have to say there's three sets of prints on the bottle. Probably the clerk in the liquor store, one set. The second set is Oliver's. I've confirmed that. Then there's another, which means he was passing the bottle. The other guy had two drinks. Well, he handled the bottle twice.'

'Then I ought to get out and talk to Oliver's uncle again. I need more detail about what happened last night.'

Stinson cleared his throat. 'I wanted to tell you something else. I'd keep this guy you sent up here on a tight rein. He's asking me if there's anything else he can do. Like I figure he'd be out there twisting Willy Veale's arm if we let him.'

'Thanks for the warning. Tell him I'll be back in town at the big tent around' – I glanced at the clock – 'seven-thirty. Ask him to see me then, could you?'

'You got it,' he said happily. 'Any word from your cameraman yet? I wondered how he made out with the shots of the truck.'

'I've been out all day, but I'll check.'

'Oh, one more thing,' he said. 'I went ahead and cancelled the truck from the wanted list. The radio and TV people monitor our frequency. A couple of them called in and asked the location so the desk man told them. They're going to get it out on the news for us, see if anyone saw Oliver.'

I thanked him and hung up the phone. I was bone weary but I saw the big brown envelope on the desk with Carl Simmons's studio stamp on the corner. I reached over for it and sat, going through the shots until the magistrate pulled in a few minutes later.

He went through the bail hearing quickly, sending the men away on their own recognizance to appear in court the following Monday. After they'd gone he had a quick word with me, tut-tutting over the way they'd hurt young Yeats. Then he closed up his briefcase and stood up. 'I hear Dancy is trying to get you fired.'

'He wants magic. And he wants it for free.'

The magistrate was a big old man, grey and experienced. 'He's got to learn to have patience,' he said. 'You've done a grand job for this place, ever since you came here. I'll have a word with him, tell him to back off a little.'

'I'd appreciate it, thank you. I've got enough on my mind without wondering where next week's pay's coming from.'

'You'll be fine,' he said. 'If what I have to say carries any weight at all.'

He left and I closed up the station and headed home. Sam was upstairs, lying outside the bathroom door. He thumped his tail on the wide old floorboards and I stooped to pat him and then looked in on Fred bathing Louise who was splashing happily in the tub.

'Go and rest,' Fred told me. 'I'll wake you in lots of time.'

It was all the invitation I needed. I slipped out of my uniform and lay on the bed, listening to the faint sounds of powerboats downstream at the lock. And the next sound I heard was Fred's voice speaking to me softly. I woke to find her sitting on the edge of the bed beside me. The light in the room had changed to the soft orange of early evening and it was streaming in the window behind her, making a red-gold halo of her hair.

I reached out for her and she came into my arms and we kissed. Then she said, 'Bad time to get romantic, old spot. The bambino's awake.'

'No sense of timing, that kid.' I let go of her.

She said: 'I've put her into her chair. We're just going. I let you sleep as long as I could.'

'What time is it? Around seven?'

She laughed. 'You're slow. It's five after. I have to head out.'

'Thanks, honey. I'll jump in the shower and see you in the big top.'

'What are you going to do?'

'What I would have done earlier if the killings hadn't happened. Talk to people, find out if anybody noticed anyone hanging around, anyone watching Amy.'

'I have to go down to Louise. If we're still here when you come down I'll tell you what I've discussed with my group.'

'Security arrangements? What?'

'Yes. Take your shower, I can be a minute or two late tonight.' She gave me a quick kiss on the forehead and pattered away downstairs. I went and showered then dressed and came down to find Fred waiting with Louise in her car seat on the floor, next to Sam who was trying not to look bored as she batted at him playfully.

The baby gave a big grin when she saw me and held out her arms. I played with her and then gave Sam a quick pat. Couldn't have him feeling left out.

Fred set out salad and a pitcher of iced tea and I sat down.

'Thanks, dear. What were you going to tell me about the cast?'

'I've had a word with a few key people. They were all alarmed, of course. More about the rape than the killings.

133

They've got the murders down as a pair of men fighting. The rapes are personal.'

'So, are they coming in convoy, what?'

'Husbands and boyfriends are driving most of them. There's about six or so living alone. They're the ones I'm worried about.'

'Have them escorted home by the other people. Either the husbands and wives, or else get Carl Simmons to go with them.'

'Good thinking. He'll do it for us. He's a sweet man.'

'Fine. I'll be there in about twenty minutes.'

Fred held up one finger. 'Oh, one other thing. Elaine Harper is coming to the rehearsal.'

'She wants to be part of the investigation, or the play?'

'She said she'll talk to you about what you want her to do, but I know that she really wants to be in the play. I'm giving her a small part, a walk on.'

I could have used Elaine better to stake out the truck at the gas station but she was a volunteer, she had to pick her own job. And it would be useful to have a trained woman watching the show from the inside. She might see things I would miss.

'That's good. Nobody needs to know she's a cop.'

'We talked about that and worked out a cover story,' Fred said. 'She's a friend from out of town, filling in for Kathie Holden.' She explained quickly. 'I'll have to get Kathie to play Hermia if Amy doesn't come back before tomorrow.'

'Sounds good. You go ahead. I'll join you down there.' I carried the baby to the car while Fred juggled her books and clipboard. Then they were gone, with a quick wave, and I went back into the house to eat and to think about the case for a few minutes.

No great inspirations came to me, but I made a mental list of the things I had to do. It was routine. Find out which men had been at the rehearsal last night, and when they had left and with whom. And had any of them seen Oliver hanging around the area? It was a cinch that he

134

had been the rapist, but I didn't think the evidence of the gloves would be enough to convict him. I needed more proof. Maybe it would emerge at the rehearsal.

It was almost dusk when I reached the marquee. Cars were parked all along Main Street, leaving barely enough room for traffic. Everyone was bustling, there was the happy, busy feeling in the air that theatricals bring out in a community. The cast was mostly young, mostly women. Fred said they were less inhibited than the men. I held the usual male opinion that women liked limelight more than we did, but when you're married to an actress you don't say things like that out loud.

I stood back for a minute or two, looking through the open flap of the tent at Fred with her clipboard of notes, running the lot of them through her intentions for the evening's rehearsal. She was wearing her Fairy Queen costume and she looked beautiful. Louise was off to one side of the stage, playing on the floor in the charge of a high-school girl in some kind of toga costume. She was acting out the part of the happy baby-sitter, doing a wonderful job, hoping for praise from Fred.

Fred saw me at the mouth of the tent and waved me in. There was a clatter of talk but it stopped when she clapped her hands. 'The chief would like to say a few words about what happened last night,' she said. That was her protocol in public, she never referred to me as her husband, always 'the chief'.

I thanked her and said: 'What happened was bad. But I have to report that Amy is going to be all right and that we have a lead on the man who did it. It's this guy, we think.' I held up the picture and they all made an actorly show of craning in for a look, as if they hadn't seen the likeness all around town.

'His name is Stuart Oliver. He's six-one, around one-seventy-five pounds, a fit, strong man in his early thirties. If you see him, don't try to hold him, even if you're as strong as George there' − I pointed to our local body-builder − 'I don't want anybody else getting hurt. But I do want your help. So I'm going to talk to you all, ask you what you remember about last night. And I'm going to ask you all to take special care going home. I think the director has some suggestions on that.' I made a gesture to Fred and she took over.

I listened while she laid out her travel suggestions and answered the inevitable questions. Then she held up her hands and said: 'OK. Tomorrow night is for the money. We've got a lot to do, so I want you to concentrate hard. Karen is going to play Hermia tonight.'

Karen was a pretty woman, a clerk in the liquor store. She blushed and Fred laughed. 'A star is born,' she said. 'Break a leg, Karen.' Then she turned to point out Elaine Harper.

'People, this is Elaine. She's a friend of mine who is going to take over in Karen's place. This is her first time in a play so let's all give her a welcome to the cast.' Everyone applauded and made welcoming noises. Elaine blushed in her turn and I hoped she would not forget what she was here to do.

Then the front flap of the marquee was closed and the bystanders began to drift away. There were more men around than I had noticed on other nights and some of them got back in their cars and left, to return later for escort duty. But a few sauntered out to the water's edge beside the tavern. Others went into the restaurant or the tavern to kill the time.

I spoke to the guys on the outside first but none of them had been around on the night before and had come now only for protection for their partners. It was the same with the men whom I followed into the restaurant and the bar. Nobody had anything useful for me and I soon came back on to Main Street and talked to the cast, keeping it informal, just chatting, seeing if they had any recollections that would help.

It was like Fred says about most of the actors she knows, they have their eyes on inside out. All they had seen was themselves and their own parts in the play and in the real-life drama, their own successes or failures. Useless as witnesses, all of them.

When I'd finished, I left them and went outside, moving around the area of the marquee, trying to put myself into the shoes of a man who could stalk and rape Amy Wilson.

It was dark by now, clear and starlit but with no moon and no streetlights, just the big bright light on the marina dock, spilling out on to the water as much as the street. The tavern and the restaurant were lit, of course, and the marquee which glowed like a jack-o-lantern with the lights inside it and gave off an attractive murmur of voices and occasional laughter.

I checked for vantage points and found that I could stand in the shadows beside the marina fence and see through a side flap of the tent into the backstage area. The cast members gathered there between scenes, waiting for their cues, chatting, unaware that they could be seen from outside. Occasionally one of the women would unselfconsciously stroke her hair or adjust a brassiere strap, innocent actions that would have been aphrodisiac to a man just out of the pen. I checked around me. The fence ended in a clump of cedars that separated the marina property from the first house up the road. Oliver could have waited there and followed Amy when she walked, unable to believe his luck that she was on foot and alone.

I had to test the theory. I went back to my car for the plastic bag containing the glove I'd found at the rape-scene. Then I ducked through the side door, surprising everyone backstage, and had one of the cast show me where Fred was.

She gave everyone a break and turned Sam over to me, and I said: 'I'll bring him back before you go home. Please don't go until I get here.'

'We'll be here till midnight. I promise,' she said. 'Louise is asleep and Elaine's watching her.'

'Fine. I'll be as quick as I can.'

Sam was delighted to be with me again and he trotted out at my heel on to the dark street. I gave him a minute to get comfortable, then put him to work. I let him sniff the glove, then led him out where I had been standing and told him to 'track'. It was a long shot. If Oliver had been here it had been twenty-four hours earlier and Sam wasn't following a proper trail, just getting a sense of his passing from where the glove had brushed the tops of the grasses along the roadside. But he found enough to work with.

I followed as he tracked along the shoulder of the road, down a couple of steps from the road surface. That made sense to me, Oliver would have walked there so he could have crouched and not be seen if Amy had turned around.

He led me all the way to Amy's house, then through the bush at the side of it, into her tiny perfect garden and up to the side of her porch. He checked there and cast around until he found the front steps. Then he bounded up, first to the side of the porch and then to her door. I stooped and made a fuss of him and told him he was a good boy. But I was thinking hard. How could Oliver have run to the porch and pulled himself on to it without Amy noticing him as she walked in from her gate? Something seemed wrong. Unless Oliver had known in advance where she lived, he wouldn't have known which house to stake out. And yet he had been waiting there for her.

I stood and thought about it all and then a car pulled up the road slowly and stopped opposite Amy's gate. A floodlight played out from it, found me and went out. Holland's voice called: 'Fred told me you'd come up here. Find anything?'

I went out to the roadway, Sam at my heel. 'If this glove is his, then he walked up here from Main Street, off the roadway and climbed in over the side of the porch.'

He leaned down on his arm. 'That's it then,' he said happily. 'Sonofabitch stalked her, raped her. Now all we've got to do is find him.'

'She said he was waiting for her when she got home.'

'So? You said yourself he came up and over the side of the porch.'

'Big question' – I held up one finger – 'how did he follow her, a stranger, and yet beat her to her own front door without her noticing?'

'Easy.' Holland snapped his fingers. 'She stood out at the gate goin': "Romeo, Romeo, wherefore art thou Romeo?" or some bullshit from the play, whatever it is. Pauses for applause, practises her bow and then comes up the walk.'

'Yeah. That's always a possibility. But it's not anything he could have counted on. Like he didn't know how long she was going to be out there.'

'Trust me. That's how it happened.' He yawned. 'Like I say, all we gotta do is find him.'

'Any news from Veale's place?'

'Nothing. I told the guys the truck was out of commission, so they're watching for him to come back on foot or in a stolen car. They'll nail him when he gets there.'

'*If* he gets there. He's got four grand in American money. To a guy like him that's enough to head for Buenos Aires.'

I leaned against the side of the car, sagging a little. It seemed we had everything we needed, except the answer. Probably Oliver had taken Amy by surprise and raped her. Probably he had then gone to the pub and had a beer. Probably he had seen Langdon's money, found him and robbed him, stabbing him into the bargain. Probably Jack McWatters had been involved and Oliver had also fought him and then knifed him for good measure. Probably.

But none of it was certain. And judges and juries didn't work on probabilities, they wanted the case proved beyond the shadow of a doubt. And I had no proof. And now, on top of everything else, I was beginning to have doubts about Amy Wilson's story.

'I still can't ride in your car with the dog, right?'

'Ah, the hell with it. Just back to the tent should be OK. Stick him in the back.'

'He'll ride in the trunk if you go slowly.'

'Naah.' He waved dismissively and I opened the rear

139

door and clicked my tongue for Sam to jump in on the seat. He did and I shut the door and got in next to Holland.

'I want to talk to the cast again. I've got an idea.'

'Gonna share?' Holland looked across at me and grinned like a kid.

'I'm wondering if Amy is having a little flirtation with one of the cast.'

'Flirtation?' He exploded with laughter. 'Is that what they're calling it these days?'

'No, that's what they called it back when she got her sex education. This is one very square little kindergarten teacher. I don't think she's the kind of girl you'd find tearing some guy's clothes off in the No-tell Motel.'

Holland laughed again. 'Romantic sonofagun, aren't you?'

'I want to check,' I said.

He dropped me at the tent, offering to come with me for the talks with the cast but I told him there was no need. 'Good,' he said. 'I promised Peg I'd be home as early as I could. How about I come back in the morning?'

I hesitated. 'I was kind of hoping we could get Veale's truck staked out. Oliver may come back and pick it up and we could get him.'

I could read Holland's resistance in his voice. 'Waste of time, if you ask me, Reid. He's ditched it, hitched a ride in a truck, stole another car, something. He's gone, like a wild goose in winter.'

Maybe yes, maybe no, but Holland wasn't going to stake out the truck, that was certain. I gave in gracefully.

'No sweat. I'd be up there, but it's my problem. So, not to worry, I'll get there later. The rape takes precedence in people's minds here. I have to show the flag.'

'See you around ten o'clock tomorrow.' We exchanged high fives and I let Sam out of the back and he backed up and picked his way out through the clutter of cars, over the bridge by the lock.

I went back over the tent and started talking to the cast and the backstage people, trying to find out if Amy had

140

been spending time with anybody in particular. It was touchy. I didn't want any rumours starting. In a small town like this, they could screw up her marriage. But I kept on until I got the impression that she had spent most of her time with the two actors who were supposed to be in love with her character in the play. Don Reynolds, who played Demetrius and Brad Stone who played Lysander.

Both of them were on stage at the time I found this out and I managed to get a moment with Fred to ask her opinion. 'Can't be Brad,' she said softly. 'He's got a new girlfriend, a nurse at Parry Sound hospital. He's loopy about her.'

'How about the lovely and talented Don Reynolds?'

She narrowed her eyes. 'He's a bit gentle. I'm not sure whether or not he's gay.'

'Carl would know.' I patted her on the arm and looked around for Carl Simmons. He was off in a corner, going over his lines with the other clowns in the cast – Fred's description – the workmen who are putting on their play within a play. The other guys, two high-school kids and an older man who kept the lock at the north end of town, were all having trouble with their lines and Carl was coaching. I extracted him and took him outside.

'Carl, nothing personal, please understand. I need your insight.'

'About what?' He sounded unusually stiff. He and I get on well but I had never initiated a conversation like this.

'Young Reynolds. Would you say he was heterosexual?'

Now he laughed and patted me on the shoulder. 'Yes. Go in peace, my son.'

'Thanks. Tell me now, second question, do you think there might be the beginning of a romance, platonic, whatever, between him and Amy Wilson?'

That made him straighten up. 'Good Lord, are you suggesting?'

'No. I'm not suggesting. I'm asking.'

He sniffed thoughtfully. 'Funny things happen on stage, even a Mickey Mouse stage like ours. You know, you could be right, she has to spend a lot of time in scenes with him. It's made them close.'

'Did he, for instance, walk Amy home last night?'

'No. He left before she did, offered a couple of people a ride but they all said no as I remember.'

'Thanks. I'd better have a word with him.'

We went back into the tent and I found Reynolds, sitting backwards on a chair, studying his script. I sat down in front of him. 'Hi. Is it hard, breaking in a new actress?'

He looked up, startled and I took stock of him. He was a lean guy of about twenty-five, reminding me a little of the actor who played the murderer in *Psycho*. Good-looking in an intense way. He was an accountant, but like a lot of guys his age, hadn't been able to find a job and was doing whatever work he could hustle up out of his parents' house in town.

'Karen's going to be fine,' he said. 'She knows her lines, but she doesn't have the timing down yet.'

'Not like Amy.' I felt like a bull in a china shop. But then, dammit, I *was* a bull in a china shop.

He narrowed his eyes, looked at me, then glanced away. 'What does that mean?'

'What it says. Not like Amy.'

It took him a little while to answer. 'She'll get there.'

A couple of people had noticed us and were pretending they hadn't, but edging closer to hear what was going on. 'Can you spare a couple of minutes, right now?' I asked him.

He looked shocked. 'For what?'

'To take a walk outside where we could talk, I wanted your opinion on something.'

He hesitated and I threw in the clincher. 'It may help me find the guy who attacked Amy.'

'In that case . . .' He closed his book and marched out. I gave him thirty seconds, then paused to chat with some-one else and followed him.

He was standing down the road a little way, between the tavern and the bridge. I went over.

142

'What did you want to know?' His voice was harsh and breathy.

'I wondered if you saw anything suspicious last night.'

'You already asked me that. I said no.'

'Since then you've had time to think.'

Now he sounded angry. 'Look, are you trying to accuse me of lying?'

'When you left last night, Amy was still here. You had asked a couple of people, including her, if they needed a ride. They all said no. Is that right?'

'Yes, that's right. You must have been asking people. Why's that?'

'Is it this play you're doing, or another one that has the line "the lady doth protest too much"?'

'Look, I came out here because you asked me to.' His voice was high and nervous. 'If you want to ask me something, please do. I've got work to do in there.'

'OK. Let me paint you a picture.' I roughened my voice deliberately, the tough cop, a role I don't play much around town. 'There's this guy, see? And he's got the hots for a girl he works with. He offers to drive her home. She knows people will talk if she says yes, so she says no. Only it's not no, it's maybe. You following this?'

'I have to get back,' he said desperately.

'Sure. So this guy thinks, right. I can take a hint. So he goes up to her place and waits for her to come home. Then she walks up. He talks to her. She says, come on in for coffee.'

He turned his head away from me, staring at the marquee, anxious to leave. I began to smell success. 'So this guy takes her hand, walks up to the porch and then, bingo! A guy is hiding there. He jumps over the rail and heads for the tall timber.'

I paused there for a moment and then roared my question. 'Is that what happened?'

A couple of the boyfriends and husbands had returned to wait for their womenfolk and they were watching us from the darkness. I knew this conversation would be replayed a hundred times by morning.

So did Reynolds. His voice was almost a bleat. 'I have to go.'

I let my voice sink almost to a whisper. 'But that's not what you said last night, is it?'

'I don't know what you mean.'

'Last night you were the big, bold saviour. And you went in for coffee and one thing led to another and then bingo!'

Now he began to sob. 'It wasn't like that,' he said brokenly. 'That's not how it happened.'

11

I softened my voice, the fatherly cop. 'Let's go somewhere private and talk.'

His shoulders shook and I led him to the police car and put him in the front seat. Not the cage. As far as the onlookers were concerned, he was a guest not a prisoner. But at the station I took him in the back way and that did what I wanted. The sight of the cells crushed him. I sat him down and brought him a glass of water. 'You didn't rape her, did you?' I said. 'The two of you made love.'

'It happened,' he said. 'It just happened. And then she started to cry and I couldn't stop her crying. She told me to get out, get out. So I went.' He sat there, drying his eyes. 'I didn't hurt her. I swear to God. She kissed me.'

I sat and thought about Amy Wilson. Petite, proper. Square. All those things. And I thought about Doug, her husband. He drove a truck but only because there weren't any teaching jobs open. He wasn't a typical blue-collar guy. He wouldn't tear Don Reynolds apart. Maybe he would walk out on Amy but I didn't think so. And knowing she had slipped a cog on her marriage vows was less than the horror of believing she had been raped.

I had no other way to play it but straight down the middle. I tapped Reynolds on the shoulder. 'Come in the office.'

He got up and went ahead of me. I switched on the light and motioned him to a chair, glancing at the clock. It was almost ten. Amy would still be up.

I had her parents' phone number in my notebook. I

dialled and a man answered, he sounded middle-aged. Her father, not her husband. 'This is Chief Bennett, Murphy's Harbour police. Is Amy Wilson there, please?'

'I hope you're phoning to say you caught that animal.'

'Could I speak to her directly, please, sir?'

The phone rustled as it was set down and I could hear wallpaper music at the other end. Then it was picked up and Amy said: 'Hello, Chief,' in a whispery voice.

'Amy. I've been talking to Don Reynolds. I want to know from you what happened.'

She gave a little gasp but said nothing. I could imagine her parents hovering around her at the other end of the line. I gave it half a minute and then said: 'You don't have to say anything, just answer yes or no to what I ask you. That be OK?'

'Yes.'

'When you came home last night, Don was waiting at your gate and you talked, right?'

'Yes.'

'So after a while, you decided to continue talking inside. So you went through the gate and up to the porch. Then this big guy who was hiding there jumped over the side and ran. Right?'

'Yes.'

'So Don said he would come in and check the house for you. You were glad of that. And he came in and one thing led to another and you made love. It was a mutual agreement. Is that right?' This was the sixty-four-dollar question. If she said no, I had to arrest Reynolds, no matter how much I believed his story.

She began to sob at the other end. 'Yes,' she said at last and then there was a clatter and the man's voice was back.

'I must protest. You've got my daughter in tears here. What's going on?'

'This will soon be ended, sir. If you would be kind enough to put her back on, please.'

A splutter of protest and then Amy's voice, calmer now. 'Hello. I'm here.'

'Thank you, Amy. Now, I know you didn't mean to be unfaithful to Doug. But when you realized what you'd done, you decided to cover it up by telling me the prowler had attacked you. Is that right?'

This time she didn't answer directly. She said: 'Am I going to be sent to prison?'

'No. The term for what you did is public mischief, but I'm not going to charge you. Nothing's going to happen. You have to explain to your husband, that's all. That ends it.'

'I'm so sorry,' she whispered. 'I've been so stupid.'

Counselling isn't my long suit. All I could think to say was: 'These things happen. I'm releasing Don, and Freda says she hopes you're back in time to take your part in the play.'

'Oh God,' she said and hung up, sobbing.

As I replaced the phone, Reynolds stood up. His expression hadn't changed. He still looked anxious. I stood there, leaning down on my desk, studying him. He had heard my statement to Amy Wilson. He knew he was off the hook for rape. So why was he so frantic to get out? A guy with more machismo might even have been swaggering a little, but he was afraid. And then I realized why.

'Sit down.' I pointed to the chair.

'But you said this was over. I heard you.'

'Sit down and shut up.'

He sat but he was babbling. 'If you're angry because I didn't come forward when the story about Amy got out, it was because I didn't want to embarrass her.'

'I said shut your mouth.' I prodded him with a rigid forefinger. He sat back in the chair, clutching the arms, his fingers rigid. 'Right, now I want you to say "tough guy". Let's hear you.'

If he had been innocent he would have done it at once. Instead he blustered. 'What's all this about? I have a right to know.'

I said nothing, just reached out and prodded him again. 'Tough guy,' I whispered.

147

He broke down. He sobbed like a baby, scrabbling in his pocket for a handkerchief.

'You thought if you kept the rapist story alive it would stop Doug Wilson from finding out that you'd screwed his wife, right?'

'I feel so bad. I'm sorry.' He was hiding among his tears like a deer in a thicket. I reached out and grabbed a handful of his hair. He stopped crying at once, gave a yelp of pain and then got to his feet as I pushed him to the back door of the office.

'Oh God. You're going to arrest me,' he wailed.

I didn't answer but walked him through to the side door which I opened. Then I shoved him through ahead of me and let him go. And as I did so I kicked him solidly in the butt. It sent him sprawling and he yelled, once, then scrambled to his feet and ran as fast as he could out into the darkness of the side road.

I didn't see him on my way back to the rehearsal. My guess was that he hid in the bush when he heard my car coming.

Nobody had left the rehearsal but there was a tension in the air that hadn't been there earlier. I had only to walk in to get Fred's attention. She came over, anxiously. 'People are saying you've arrested Don Reynolds.'

'No. He's free and clear. But Amy has dropped the rape charge and the affair is closed. Can you think of some clever way of letting people know without saying out loud that she and Reynolds were playing mom and pop?'

'I think we just say she's dropped the charges. That plus the sight of Don in your car will give them the rest of the story.'

'Yes, and there's one other thing. He's the guy who phoned you and talked dirty. He was doing it to stokc up the rape story.'

Fred frowned. 'That was a bad thing to do, it's made me just about sick to my stomach with worry.'

'Remember what I said I'd do to him?'

She was wearing stage make-up and when she raised

her eyebrows her green eyes were as big as saucers.

'You didn't?'

'Not in the equipment, but he'll eat his supper off the mantelpiece tomorrow.'

She said: 'I guess I shouldn't be pleased, but I'm relieved as all getout.'

'I guess. He only did it to keep Doug Wilson from suspecting that he and Amy had gone the distance.'

Now she laughed out loud. 'You've got more alternative expressions for making love than anybody in the world.'

'I could have been Shakespearean and said they were making the beast with two backs.' I felt almost giddy with relief that the threat against Fred had been lifted.

She bumped me on the shoulder, laughed and got up on stage. The cast fell silent immediately and she made a brief announcement. 'Good news, people. We don't have a rapist in our midst. Amy has told the chief that she wasn't raped. The whole thing was a mistake.'

That made everybody buzz but she held up her hands and went on. 'I know we're all wondering what did happen. I am, just as much as you. But let's be adults about this. Let's keep our questions and suspicions to ourselves and let's not make Amy feel out of place or uncomfortable when she gets back. How does that sound?' She looked around as if she expected an answer and then clapped her hands. 'OK. So you know where we were. Let's get on with it or we'll be here all night.'

Somebody said, 'Don's not here and he's in this scene.'

'I'll read Demetrius's part,' Fred said. 'Places, please.'

Reynolds's absence made the buzzing start again but it subsided and people took their places for the scene.

I watched for a few moments then went back to my car. Solving the rape case had taken the steam out of me. Reynolds had made the whole thing personal when he made his phone call. Now the threat was gone and I only had the murderers to worry about. Sure, they were bigger crimes, but they were in the same league as cyclones or

149

earthquakes. Some outside force had come into town, done the damage and gone. It was less of a threat.

I sat in the car for a while, trying to get my head around the killings, trying to pick up momentum again. No brilliant insights came to me so I went and asked more questions.

The cashier at the Lakeside Tavern pointed out a couple of parties who had been there the same time the previous night and I talked to them. Had they noticed anything unusual when they left? Had they seen a pickup truck driving north past the tavern. They hadn't so I went on to the Murphy's Arms.

The Blue Jays were doing it to Detroit on the big TV and I had a tough time getting anyone's attention. But one by one I worked my way through the crowd, asking what they had seen that might be helpful to me.

A lot of them could give me a blow-by-blow account of the fight, but nothing useful. And then I came to a table of three young guys. Two of them were locals, the third was a stranger to me, and they all looked nervous when I reached their table. At least one of them was under age was my guess. They were drinking the latest fad beer, ice-beer, overproof. It was another hint that they were too young to be legal.

There was a spare chair at their table and I sat down with them. 'Hi, guys. What's your names?' That pumped up the tension some more and then I gave them the easy questions. Had they been in the night before? What had they noticed?

The two older boys did most of the talking. They were barely nineteen, I judged, anxious to please. They had seen nothing useful. But the other one had, I could tell. Maybe because coming to a bar was new to him, he had noticed everything that happened. He wasn't going to say anything but I asked him directly.

He cleared his throat, nervously. 'Well, I don' know's it's important.'

'Try me.'

'Like, we all wen' out after the fight, couple minutes later.'

'Yes.'

'Well, there was this big Buick outside. Two guys in. One o' them came in here. Then he come out again an' they left, like before we was off the lot.'

'A Buick? Did you get a good look at the men? Or the car? Would you recognize them again?'

'Can't say as I would.' He shook his head. Then he smiled, remembering. 'Oh, yeah. Like it was an American plate on it. Not Ontario.'

'What state, do you remember?'

He pulled his eyebrows down. 'No. But, one thing. Like I told the guys about it.'

'What was that?'

He chuckled. 'Well like, here they was goin' in the bar, an' on their bumper they had all these like God stickers. Ya know?'

Yes. I knew. I'd seen a car with an American plate and religious bumper-stickers, parked outside the Bonanza Motel, the unit the Whelans were occupying. The only thing was, they had told me they had stayed there at the motel, waiting for Langdon to return. Why had they lied?

I got the boys' names and phone numbers and headed up to the Bonanza Motel to talk to the Whelans again. My head was buzzing with the questions I was going to ask but as I passed the Shell station where Veale's pickup had been left I glanced over and then slammed on the brakes and wheeled in. The trailer that had been parked there was gone. And so was the pickup.

I got out of the car and swore. I should have been here. Oliver had come and gone and I'd missed him. I swore once more and looked around. The lights at the pump island and in the office were out. The couple who ran the place had gone. I wondered if they had seen Oliver come back. Maybe they had, but I'd missed the call, out at the rehearsal, solving the rape. Maybe Dancy was right. I couldn't do this job on my own. The OPP should take over. At least they had the manpower to cover the kind of case load I had right now.

I checked all around the lot, making sure the truck was gone for sure. Then I used the phone box beside the shack to call the OPP. The guy on the desk was a new transfer. I'd never met him and he treated me as if I were a house-holder with a missing cat. I contained myself and asked if he could pass my message on to the Emergency guys at Veale's place.

'They're not there any more.'

'Where have they gone?'

'Don't you watch the news?'

'We're making news down here, not watching it. I'm in the middle of a double homicide investigation. Where have they gone?'

'Jesus. Keep your shirt on,' he grunted in disgust. I waited and finally he said: 'There's a guy holding his wife hostage on a farm down in Cromwell county.'

'And there's nobody assigned to the Veale place?'

The cares of office were heavy on his back. 'We got hardly enough guys to cover routine duties.'

'Thanks. Please get this truck on the air. Stop and approach with caution. It's probably being driven by Oliver.' I was annoyed enough to get in a little dig. 'You'll have heard about him if you watched the news before you came on.'

'I read the report.'

'Good. That's one thing. And there's a second, and it's important. Got a pencil?'

'Sure, shoot.'

'Make a note that I am going up to the Veale camp now. If I get away and back to my station without any problems, I'll call you. Otherwise, ask your relief to let your desk sergeant know I've gone up there. Can you do that?'

'OK.' He sounded puzzled. 'I can do it, but what for?'

'Think about it.' I hung up and frowned at the phone. This was not the smartest thing I had ever done, but I had to go back to Veale's bear camp right now and check whether Oliver had returned. I needed Sam but I wasn't about to take him away from Fred. Sure the threat to her had been cancelled, but Oliver was loose and he was dangerous. He had tracked Amy Wilson down the night before. He might try it again with another woman, and my wife was the best-looking woman in town. I couldn't leave her and Louise undefended.

It took thirty-five minutes to get to the camp. On the way I had debated the ways of approaching the cabin. The sneaky choice was to leave my car down the track and go in on foot. But the memory of Veale's dog killed that one. He would pick up my scent and alert the whole camp before I could get close. Surprise was out of the question. I had to do it like the cavalry in a cowboy movie, ride right in, prepared to fight. So I drove up, fast, lights blazing, right around the back of the cabin.

Veale's little Chevy truck was parked in his garage.

I spun my car around and shone the floodlight in through the window. I could hear his dog bellowing with fury in the cabin, scrabbling at the heavy door as I slid out of the car, picking up the microphone. I crouched, switching on the PA. 'This is the police. We have the house surrounded. If you try to run we will shoot. Secure your dog inside the cabin and come out with your hands up.'

There was a long pause, then the door scraped open and the dog burst out and charged me, bellowing with fury. I played the floodlight into his eyes and they glowed like the fires of hell as he bounded at me, jaws wide. Then I shot him right between the eyes and he fell out of the air, folding and flopping at my feet, not even having time to whimper.

There was a yell of fury from the cabin and I dropped the floodlight and rolled sideways as a gun boomed twice, a big gun, rifle or shotgun, shattering the glass in my cruiser.

Instinctively I put two shots into the darkness, three feet back from the muzzle flash. My ears were ringing

153

from the gunshots but I still heard the clatter of the falling gun.

I kept low, crabbing over to the wall of the cabin where nobody could shoot me out of the window. The shots had deafened me and my eyes weren't accustomed to the dark so I waited, listening intently, straining to see.

There was no movement and after about half a minute I took out my flashlight and stood up, silently, not turning it on. Still there was no shot. No sound. But I didn't take chances. I went right around the side of the cabin to the front door. It was open and I waited for a long moment, gathering my courage, then burst through it, taking a step to one side and crouching.

Still no sound. I stayed low, behind the table for a moment, then flicked on my flashlight. There was a man lying in the back doorway. His eyes were open and there was blood in his mouth. I flashed my light around the cabin, standing up now but keeping the light at arm's-length out to my side. Anybody aiming at the light would have missed me by a yard.

Both the beds were disturbed. There had been other men here. But now there was only one, and he was dead.

I flicked my light over the gun rack. The rifle and shotgun were missing. I guessed that the dead man had used one of them. It was by the back door. But that left another gun, and at least one other man outside somewhere, maybe waiting for me to step out and show a light so he could put a bullet through me.

I switched off my light and went to the man on the floor and felt for a pulse. There was none. The shotgun was lying beside him. I pulled it into the cabin, then picked him up under the arms and dragged him inside.

I shoved the door closed with my heel and shone my light on the dead face. I was expecting Veale, or Oliver. But this man was a stranger, in his thirties, small and lean, with long blond hair. He was wearing a T-shirt with two bloodstained holes in the chest, almost under his left arm. On the arm there were a couple of poorly executed tattoos.

154

I've seen enough of them to recognize jailhouse work. This was a penitentiary buddy of Oliver's.

I left him and went into the smaller bedroom. There was a pair of blue jeans on the floor with a billfold in the pocket. In it there was a driver's licence in the name of Murray Corbett. It told me he was thirty-six and lived in Sudbury. It had been issued six months earlier.

He also had a horse-choking wad of bills, loose in his right-hand pocket. I counted eight hundred and change, mostly in tens and twenties. Part of Thad Langdon's money? For sure a guy like Corbett would never have had money like this on him legally. Not unless he'd won the sweep. It explained why he had set the dog on me, and then fired. He had to be involved in some heist. Maybe he had been with Oliver when he killed Langdon. He knew I'd be asking questions and he'd reacted in panic, trying to blast his way out, knowing he wouldn't get any longer in jail for killing me than for his part in the other homicides.

That theory fit. It meant that perhaps he had been the other guy with Oliver in the pickup before the rape. It could be that his were the fingerprints on the whisky bottle. And maybe he drove McWatters's pickup up to the Cassidys' while Oliver drove his own vehicle. And then they had dumped McWatters's body in the lake and taken off. It all fit perfectly.

I was excited by the thought, but I checked the cabin carefully. There weren't any other clothes on the floor in either room. I clicked off my light and tried to picture what had happened when I got here. Veale and Oliver must have been away, maybe in the bush, baiting bears? Or maybe they had heard me coming, grabbed their clothes and run out, taking the other gun, waiting to nail me. That was a scary thought, but it didn't fit. They would have been close enough to shoot me after Corbett had fired. No, they had to be away somewhere else.

That thought made me a little easier in my mind. But

I knew that if they were close enough to hear the shots they would come back. I was still a target.

I studied the situation tactically, as if I were back in Nam. The cabin was a trap. I had to get out so I took the shotgun with me and crept through the front door, moving silently around the cabin, keeping low. It was too dark to see anything more than the tops of trees against the sky but I didn't hear anything moving so I went to the car and switched on the radio, holding the mike and lying flat beside the car as I used it.

It was no good. Fifteen years earlier, when the previous chief had installed it, my radio had been state of the art. But its range was limited and I was on the outer fringe of my area.

I called the station but there was no response and I tossed the mike on the seat and lay still, listening for movement in the bush. Nothing stirred but I've been in spots like this before, I knew they could be waiting to lull me until they had a clear shot so I played safe, squirming away from the car, on my belly to the edge of the trees and waited there for someone to make a move.

Again, nobody did and I began to accept the fact that Corbett had been alone in the camp. The others might have heard the gunshots but if they tried to get back here in a hurry they would make noise. For the moment all I had to do was wait.

I used the time to put Corbett's shotgun into the trunk of my car and to unlock my own from its rack in the front seat. Then I ripped the plug leads out of the pickup truck and flung them into the trees. Not clever, but I could do it in the dark and it would be enough to keep them here.

After that there was nothing to do but scout the area as well as I could without using my flashlight. I found a track, out behind the icehouse, leading off into the trees. If they had gone into the bush, that was the path they had used, the way they would come back. It made me stop and move my car around to the front of the shack.

They would not see it there, I would have an extra second or two to take them.

I went back to the track and checked it again. It was too enclosed to make a good ambush spot. They could have dived into the bush and been gone within seconds. I had to be where they could see that I had the drop on them with the shotgun. That was the only way I might be able to bring them in without shooting.

I picked a spot on the edge of the clearing at the back of the house and sat and reloaded my service revolver. It left me with a full load and three shots over. That plus the five shells in my shotgun. Not much fire power if things got noisy. I had to hope they wouldn't. But I was grateful for the problem. It took my mind off Corbett's body lying twenty yards away in the darkness.

I sat there, reliving the shot he had fired at me, weighing my response, my trained response to put him down before he could shoot again. I remembered the anger in the eyes of the dog and knew that Corbett's anger must have been just as strong. I'd had no choice but to stop him, and now he was dead, with all his undischarged anger hanging in the air around us. The thought made the hair prickle on my neck.

I got restless, wondering if Oliver or his uncle might be hiding somewhere close, waiting until their eyes grew accustomed to the dark before they drew a bead on me. It made me tense enough that I worked my way all round the cabin again, not switching on my light but making doubly sure I was alone.

I covered it all and came back to my spot by the ice-house. But the feeling persisted so I opened the door, ducking to one side and crouching instantly. It was pitch black in there, and I had to use my flashlight, masking the beam with my fingers, letting only a glimmer of light through as I checked around.

There was nobody there but I realized that the drum with the bear bait in it had been moved since I saw it last. I propped the shotgun against my leg and checked it more closely, letting a touch more light leak out from the flashlight between my fingers.

I could see bloodstains and when I shone more light on them I saw they were smeared. Someone had wiped with a wet rag, but there was enough blood left to show that the stains were fresh.

It didn't make sense. The OPP team that had been here earlier would have kept Veale where they could see him. He wouldn't have been out here, chopping something up. And when I was here I hadn't seen any carcasses to be chopped. Just who had been cutting up what? And was it important to me?

I stood there, with a sliver of light coming out between my fingers and then an even smaller glint of light was reflected back from the trampled earth beside the drum. I stooped and touched the brightness and found it was a clip-on pearl earring.

Automatically I glanced over my shoulder at the door, then stooped and picked up the little bead and studied it, in the same narrow chink of light through my fingers. There was a dark spot on the gold of the clip and I recognized it instantly as blood.

12

I tore out a page from my notebook and wrapped the pearl in it then stowed it and the book back in my shirt pocket and prised the lid off the drum.

It seemed the same, part full of grocery-store plastic bags, knotted, slimy to the touch. I slipped out my pocket-knife and slashed the topmost package. It held a chunk of meat about six inches long, with a big bone running through it. The bone had been cut roughly, with a chopper, not a saw.

There was no skin on the meat, it might have been anything, but I couldn't help thinking it was part of a human thigh.

I put the lid back on the drum and switched off the light, turning to face the open door and standing where I was until my night vision had recovered to where I could make out the opening against the deeper darkness of the inside of the shed. Then I came back out, staying low, ready to shoot at once if anything moved.

Nothing did. An owl was whiffling away in the trees behind me but that was all. No other sound. I found my way back to the same tree I had chosen before and leaned against it to wait.

They came back two hours later. I was standing against the same tree, fighting off sleep when I heard footsteps on the track, trudging, weary footsteps, no caution to them, they hadn't heard the shooting. I slipped behind the tree trunk and raised the shotgun. They came around the corner of the icehouse and headed for the shack.

I heard Veale say: 'Goddamn dog's asleep,' and the other man mumble something.

I shouted: 'Police! Hold it right there!' and flashed my light on them.

It works sometimes, you jacklight people, they freeze, the way a deer will freeze. But Veale wasn't that slow. He shouted: 'It's cops! Run, Stu!'

'Hold it there!' I cut the light and fired in the air above them. The second man ran, diving back behind the icehouse to safety. But Veale whipped his rifle to his hip and fired twice.

He missed and I dropped to one knee and yelled: 'Drop the gun!' But he fired again, the slug slamming into the trunk of the tree that sheltered me, making it twang like a tuning fork. I had no choice. I fired, but in the microsecond before I pulled the trigger I lowered the gun to the level of his feet.

He screamed and fell, writhing. I dashed to him and grabbed his rifle, then ran off behind the icehouse and into the pathway I'd found. Branches whipped my face and I slowed and listened but heard nothing. If Oliver had started off by running, he had stopped now, sunk down out of sight maybe, waiting to grab me as I blundered into range.

Without Sam to search for him it was hopeless. Walking down that trail would have been committing suicide.

I turned back and went to the clearing where Veale was rolling on the ground, rocking, holding his feet, crying in pain. I gave him a quick flash of light and saw that his feet were a mass of blood from the ankles down. I ran to the cruiser and backed it up around the shack and alongside him. He was still screaming and I picked up the floodlight and flashed it around to make sure Oliver was nowhere close.

I couldn't see him so I switched off all the lights, grabbed Veale by the collar and heaved him into the cage of the cruiser. Then I slung the rifle and my shotgun into the front seat and hauled out of there as hard as I could, lights blazing.

Veale was screaming with pain but I took no notice until I was out on the side road, too far away for Oliver to reach me while I got the first-aid kit from the trunk and did my best for Veale.

I slashed the laces on his boots, and then the leather as well when he screamed as I tried to remove them. I poured Mercurochrome on the wounds and stuck dressings on and lashed them roughly but tight. He was trying to get out of the car, swearing at me in a high, shrill voice, but I shoved him back in the cage, flat-handed, and drove out on to the highway and up to the hospital at Parry Sound.

There was no traffic and I made it in twenty minutes, without using my siren. The nurse in the emergency ward was half asleep but within a minute she had the doctor there and they rushed Veale into a trauma room.

I walked back to the reception area and sat down, wearily. The hard part was about to begin. Slowly I dialled the OPP.

The same dough-head was on the desk but I shut him up and asked for the duty inspector. Inspector is a management rank, equivalent to maybe captain in an American department. I was lucky, the duty man was a guy called Banner, a cop's cop.

I kept my language formal. 'Inspector. This is Reid Bennett, Murphy's Harbour. I've been involved in two shoot-outs, concerning the murder investigation in my jurisdiction.'

'Two separate shoot-outs?'

'Yes. Both at the same place. Veale's bear camp. It's on a logging road, in from side road sixteen of Calvin township.'

'What happened?'

I gave him the *Reader's Digest* version. He listened and then asked: 'You're at the emergency entrance, Parry Sound Hospital?'

161

'Yes, I am.'

'Stay there, please. I'll be over.'

He hung up and I sat back and the next thing I knew the doctor was shaking me awake. 'Officer. Are you all right?'

I blinked at him. 'Yes, it's been a long night, I dozed.'

He licked his lips nervously. 'The OPP has to hear about this, you know that, don't you?'

I blinked. 'It's done. Inspector Banner of the local detachment is on his way over.'

He was a young guy, a Mennonite, judging by the shape of his beard. They're one of the pacifist Christian sects, good people but they sure don't understand police work. 'This man may lose his right foot. Was it necessary to shoot him?'

'He was trying to kill me, Doctor. I should have blown his head off but I didn't. He's lucky, if you can believe it.'

He reached out his hand and I flinched but he took my wrist and counted. 'Your heartbeat's very high,' he said. 'You need help yourself.'

'I'm OK. It's combat fatigue, soldier's heart, something.'

'I'll give you a sedative when you leave. Take it when you get home and get some sleep. You're exhausted.'

'Thank you, Doctor. Right now, I'd settle for a cup of coffee, hot and black.'

He gave a short humph of laughter. 'Not what I'd pre-scribe, but very well. I'll ask the nurse to bring you one.'

It was the same nurse who had been in the delivery room the night my wife had the baby. She didn't bother asking why I'd shot Veale, just set down the coffee cup and said: 'Holler if you'd like more. I'll be down the hall with that guy.'

'Thanks. This is great.'

I sipped and waited and soon Banner arrived. I made an effort to stand but he waved me down. 'Relax, skip the formalities. How are you feeling?'

'Tired, but better than the other two guys.'

162

'We're going to have to go out there and check the site,' he said. 'You up to that?'

'I'm fine. But there's something else – I didn't tell you on the phone, but it's important.'

'What's that?'

I felt in my pocket for the pearl earring. 'Do you have any reports of assaults on women not accounted for yet?' I found the sheet of paper and unfolded it to show him the pearl. 'This was up at Veale's camp, lying beside a barrel he stores bad meat in to bait his bears. It wasn't there this morning.'

Banner didn't touch it. He reached into his pocket for a gold pencil and used the tip to turn the earring over. 'That looks like blood.'

'That's what I thought. There were fresh bloodstains on the barrel where they store the meat. They've cut up a carcass since I was up there this morning.'

Banner looked at me, his eyes not quite focused. 'Mother of God,' he whispered. 'They've cut her up and fed her to the animals.'

'Cut who up?'

'There was a hold-up at a donut shop on the highway near Point Au Baril. The clerk was raped, money stolen. As the two guys left a woman was coming in. They grabbed her, shoved her into her car and drove off.'

'Who was she?'

He shook his head. 'We don't know. Nobody's been reported missing, it only happened last night, around ten. The clerk saw it happen but she didn't get a good look at the woman, nor the car. She was in shock anyways. All she could say was the woman was young and wearing a kind of a business suit.'

'Some sales rep maybe, travelling on business.'

'Sounds like it. The clerk says she had enough moxie to scream and shout "Call nine-one-one" and then they threw her into the back seat of her car and drove off. The big guy got in with her.'

I checked him. 'This twosome, big guy, little guy?'

163

'Yes. The little guy had the gun. He waved it around a lot, acted tough. The big guy was the one who twisted the clerk's arm until she opened the cash box, then he dragged her out to the kitchen and raped her.'

'That's Oliver and the guy I shot, Corbett.' I felt in my pants pocket for Corbett's wallet and money.

Banner looked at it and whistled. 'You count this?'

'Eight hundred and change. His half of the donut shop money.'

Banner nodded. 'And then bloodstains and an earring at the place where you found Corbett. Sounds like they're the guys from the donut shop, and also they've killed this other poor bloody woman.'

'If we're right, then Oliver has to be the dumbest sonofabitch in history. Either that or the guy with the most chutzpah. Veale must have told him the ERT boys had been there all day, yet he took the time to dispose of the body. It doesn't make sense.'

'Crime never does, until you realize that half of the guys who do it don't like being on the outside. They'd rather be in the pen. It explains why they act so dumb.'

I stood up. 'Let's talk to Veale. He's just down the hall.'

'Yeah. Let's do that, but don't come right out with the business about the woman. Just take it one step at a time.'

'You do it, I'll just talk about my homicides.'

We walked down the hall and tapped on the door of the treatment room. The nurse opened it and we went in. She looked at us and said, 'I have to get some dressings. I'll be three minutes.'

'Thank you, nurse,' Banner said. He closed the door behind her and spoke to Veale.

'You're goddamn lucky it's your toes got shot, not your head.'

I had expected lies, bluster, but instead Veale said simply: 'I know. I'm sorry I shot at the off'cer.'

'You'll be charged with attempted murder. But I'll take this comment into consideration and see what I can do for you at the trial,' Banner said grimly. 'One of my men

164

will come in and caution you and read you your rights. If you change your story and tell lies about this officer you're going down for attempted murder.'

'Don't worry,' Veale lay back. 'I been talkin' to Stu since he got out. I sure as hell don't wanna do no time in the pen.'

'Maybe you won't,' Banner said. 'Not if you help us. Now, what were you doing in the bush last night?'

'Workin'.' Veale put his hand over his eyes to shade them.

'At what?' Banner's voice was contemptuous. 'I'm not some city boy, I grew up here. Nobody goes into the bush at night to work.'

'We was baitin',' Veale said. 'I got a party comin' in day after tomorrow. Had to be done when we done it. Any later the bears'd've not been hungry.'

'Listen,' Banner said. 'I'm a hunter. Nobody baits bears at night.'

Veale shrugged. It was a sure sign he was lying but he didn't care. 'I do. I bait 'em when I get the chance. Last night I had the chance.'

I drilled a question at him. 'Why did you tell Oliver to run when I spoke to you? Had he told you about killing those two men?'

'No.' Veale shut his mouth like a trap.

'Did it have anything to do with the fact that his buddy Corbett had eight hundred dollars in his pocket when I found him?'

That made Veale react. He said: 'Waddya mean, found him? Where is he?'

'He's at your camp.'

Banner said: 'Eight hundred and change. That's half the money was taken in that donut shop heist last night.'

Veale was about to ask more questions but he clamped his mouth shut again when he heard that. Bingo! We had solved the donut store robbery.

'Two men. One of them tall, answering Oliver's description. The other, well, suppose you tell me what he looked like, Officer.'

I gave a quick rundown and Banner smiled. 'That's the little bastard who cleaned out the cash while the big guy raped the clerk. They got sixteen hundred and forty-eight dollars.'

'Why did you leave him in the camp?' I kept my voice quiet, the reasonable cop, not so uptight as Banner.

Veale had regained his control. 'They din' say nothin' 'bout no hold-up. Stu was out, he come back with the little guy, said he was a buddy. I din' mind. So, me'n Stu went out baitin'. The little guy didn' like the bush at night. So we left him there in the camp, with the dog for company.'

'And you left him the shotgun. Why?'

Veale looked at me, beginning to understand. 'He take a shot at you?'

'Yes. That was right after I shot the dog.'

'Where is he? The little guy?' Veale's voice was fearful.

'He's at your place.'

'You arrested him, right?'

'He's dead,' Banner said angrily. 'He shot at this officer, he returned fire and your guy is up there with a hole in him.'

Veale covered his face. 'Oh Jesus, Mary and Joseph. Stu's gonna kill you for this. He'll kill you sure.'

13

The nurse came in and told us she had to put a new dressing on Veale's feet. She didn't exactly kick us out but we took her hint and went back to the office.

Banner did the talking. 'This has to be done right. The Hold-up Squad is handling the donut shop case. They work out of the Bracebridge detachment. I'm going to pass them the investigation of this earring and the possibility that the woman was killed and cut up at Veale's place.'

'How about the investigation of the guy I shot at the camp?'

He shook his head. 'They don't touch that. I'll handle it. They may want you suspended until the investigation's over. We can't afford that, we need everyone out looking for this guy Oliver. He's an animal.'

I said nothing and he went on, almost to himself: 'I can cut through the bull faster than they will.' He stood for a few seconds, in silence, then said: 'Just hold on a spell. I have to get a man here to guard Veale.'

When the patrol car arrived with the officer to guard Veale we drove back to Banner's office. He got all the new developments on the air and then called in extra men from other detachments to search the bush at Veale's cabin.

After that he took a statement from me, then collected the rifle and shotgun I'd taken off Veale and Corbett. The shotgun had been modified illegally. The plug that closed the magazine down to the legal three shells had been removed and although Corbett had fired it twice there was still one shot in the chamber and two more in the

167

magazine. Banner made a note of that and set the gun aside to be fingerprinted.

The rifle still held two rounds, and he agreed with a nod that it had been fired. 'Won't mean a thing to the media,' he reminded me. 'If they take a dislike to you they're still liable to suggest that you could have fired it, after you'd plugged Corbett.'

I didn't argue. We both knew the words and music of that song. I sometimes figure that you need a major Oedipus complex to get hired as a journalist. Most of them slam the hell out of anybody in uniform. As a cop you just grit your teeth and remember the old saying, if you can't take a joke, you shouldn't have joined.

It was only five a.m. but Banner hauled Dave Stinson out of bed to photograph my car with its buckshot damage and when Dave arrived, bleary-eyed, half an hour later, Banner co-opted him to come up to Veale's camp with the two of us and a senior detective.

By now it was around six so I phoned Fred. She'd had a quiet night but was wondering where I was. I kept the news as neutral as possible but told her I was looking for Oliver and that she should keep Sam with herself and the baby at all times. She could read between the lines of the request and I heard a touch of fear in her voice, but she didn't argue, just kept it light and told me she would be in town most of the day, at the marquee. The play opened that evening and she had a raft of details to attend to. That suited me just fine. She'd be safe in a crowd, with Sam at her side, keeping watch.

We set off for Veale's place just as it was getting light. I drove my own car with its missing windows. Fortunately, it was a warm morning and I didn't mind the wind howling in.

It was broad daylight when we got there. Banner's car was right behind me and he and Stinson and the detective got out and we all walked around the cabin.

Veale's pickup truck was still there and the dead dog

was lying where it had dropped. But it was no longer tumbled in a heap, the way it had died.

I unflipped my holster and looked around quickly. 'Oliver's been back. He's moved the dog. Keep your eyes open.'

Banner said: 'Stinson, look in the cabin. And watch yourself. These guys had a gun when they robbed the donut shop. It's not been recovered.'

Dave turned away and I took the other buildings, checking in and around the garage first, then the icehouse. There was nobody there and I stood at the icehouse door and checked all around, as far as I could see into the bush. No sign of Oliver. If he was still here he was well hidden. If I'd had Sam along I could have found him in minutes, but I didn't, and I was glad he was protecting my family.

The OPP men were bending over Corbett's body. It had been covered with a blanket and Stinson had pulled it back to reveal the wounds in the chest.

'Two shots inside a three-inch circle.' Banner looked at me, eyes narrowing. 'How far away was he when you fired?'

'About forty feet. Come outside, you'll see.'

He followed me out and I showed him where I'd been crouching, at the back of my car. 'I was here. I'd just shot the dog, then I set the floodlight down on the hood of the car and rolled back here.'

'Good thing you did,' Banner said absently. He was prodding through the dry grass with his toe until he found what he was looking for. He stooped and fingered the spot, showing me what he had found, granulated glass. 'This must've come from your window.'

'Most of it was blown into the car, you saw that.'

'This locates you.' He stood up. You're right. You were about forty feet from the doorway. You say he fired from there.'

'Opened the door and – bang!'

He went to the doorway and glanced around his feet, then took out his pen and stooped to lift an empty shotgun

169

shell on the end of it. He stood at the door, one foot advanced, hands extended as if he were aiming a gun at the spot where he had found the glass. He kept his arm raised and glanced at me; I was standing in the place from which I'd fired.

'You're a damn good shot if you hit him from that distance.'

'That's a matter of record, Inspector. The Marine Corps gave me better weapons training than they dish up at the academy. My marksmanship scores have always been high.'

'It sure paid off last night.' He raised one finger to keep me in my spot, then went into the cabin briefly. He came out without the shotgun shell, poking his pen back into his pocket.

'Right. Now tell me about this second guy, Veale. Where were you when he shot at you?'

I walked him through the exchange with Veale and he looked around for Veale's shells, then examined the tree his bullet had hit and shook his head bemusedly. 'I'd say you're up to quota on excitement for a while. You could've been killed here.'

I looked at the scarred tree. 'If he'd been the one using the shotgun, I'd have been in real trouble.'

He shook his head. 'He's goddamn lucky you didn't blow him away. Hell, he deserved it.'

'Let's hope the media feels the same way, Inspector.'

That angered him. 'The hell with those people. We have a legal system in this country, if the law says you did right, you did right no matter what some snot-nosed reporter thinks.'

We heard cars on the logging road and walked to the corner of the cabin. An OPP car and a civilian four-by-four were rolling up the driveway. They stopped and the guys got out. They were dressed in uniform shirts and pants but you could tell these were old clothes, they weren't about to go into the bush looking as if they were heading

170

out on parade. They had shotguns with them, as well as service revolvers.

I didn't know any of them so I stood back while Banner briefed them as they pulled on their bullet-proof vests. The guy in the four-by-four had a dog with him, some kind of setter. That was good, even an ordinary hunting dog would give them an edge when they were poking through the bush. He would cut Oliver's chance of hiding out or sneaking past them.

Banner warned them about that possibility. I heard him say: 'Be sure there's a man here at all times. The guy you're after has spent time in these woods. He's quite capable of getting through your line of advance and coming back here to take a vehicle and head out.'

They assured him that one of them would stay and then moved out towards the trail. We watched them go and then Banner said: 'OK, Bennett. I'll make this official on a fax to you when I get back to my office. But I'm telling you that my preliminary investigation shows that you acted with due care in the use of your weapon. I will recommend that you're not suspended from duty.' And then, surprisingly, he reached out to shake my hand.

'Thanks, Inspector, I appreciate it.'

He nodded. 'I understand your reeve is making noises about having our guys police Murphy's Harbour.' He hooked his thumb back over his shoulder at the scene of the shootings. 'I'm goddamn glad we didn't have one of our rookie officers here. I'd be arranging a police funeral.'

He turned away to talk to his men and I headed out, gratefully. I kept my eyes peeled along the logging road in case Oliver was making his way out but I saw nothing and was soon zipping down the highway to the Harbour.

The two cars from Virginia were still parked outside the Bonanza Motel and on impulse I swung in there and pulled up in front of the Whelan unit.

George came to the door, carrying his bible. He looked at me oddly and I realized that after my night in the bush

171

and all the adventures I'd been through since I saw him last, I looked less than neat. 'Yes, Officer?' he said.

I threw the question at him without warning. 'Tell me what you were doing down at the tavern the night your cousin was killed.'

The question was beyond his ability to answer. He turned around and his brother spoke for him. 'You're forgetting, Officer, we already told you, we didn't go to the tavern after I had dropped Thad there.'

'I have a witness who saw you there.'

Roy shook his head. 'I'm sorry, this so-called witness is mistaken, Officer.'

'I'm sorry too, but I'm going to have to question you further about this. You'll have to attend a line-up with my witness present.'

Roy looked at me calmly. 'My brother and I do not tell falsehoods, Officer. I realize you find this hard to believe, but it's a simple truth.'

Behind him the door opened wider and Langdon appeared. 'You still sayin' my cousins were down the bar just before Thad was knifed?'

I kept it simple. 'Yes.'

'I bin talkin' to them about that. They tell me they weren't. I've never known 'em tell anythin' but the truth.'

I shrugged. 'In that case they have nothing to fear from my line-up. I'll get back to you with the time and place. Do not leave this area until it's over or I'll have you picked up.'

Langdon sneered. 'That the best you can come up with? Can't find the guy'd killed Thad so you're blamin' his kin?'

He was back to the same level of truculence he'd brought to town. Puncture time again.

'Did you know your kid brother carried a concealed weapon?'

He pulled back. 'Not a goddamn gun?'

'Not a goddamn gun, no. A Tennessee toothpick, in a sheath down his back. Did you know that?'

He backed off some more on this one. 'Not in town he didn't. Just in the bush.'

'He wore it down the Murphy's Arms. The sheath was found on his body when the forensic people made the search. The sheath but not the knife.'

'Then he likely left it around here before he went out.' Langdon was frowning, thinking hard as he answered.

'Sure, and left the sheath hanging down his neck, empty. Right? And if he did, where is it? It's not with his gear, I went through that.'

Now Roy rounded out the chorus with his bass voice. 'Are you suggesting he was murdered with his own knife, Officer?'

'Can any one of you describe it for me?'

The brothers looked at one another and frowned. Langdon said: 'I sure can. I made the goddamn thing for him, for his birthday one year. It's got a ten-inch blade, inch and a half wide at the hilt, down to a point, mahogany handle with three copper rivets. Why'd you wanna know?'

'Because that's the knife that was used to kill the other victim. We found it.'

'You sayin' Thad did that? You sayin' he killed that guy, then stabbed himself and walked back to the place where he was found and died. You outa your mind?' Langdon was shouting now, froth forming at the corners of his mouth.

I stood and stared at him without speaking until he got himself under control. 'There's a lot of questions need answers. Please don't leave town until I've had a chance to arrange the line-up.'

I nodded and left the three of them standing in the doorway as I went back to my car. I had to back away and I saw Langdon staring at the damage to the right side. He knew bullet holes when he saw them and I wondered what he was making of these.

We have a body-shop on the edge of town: body-shop, garage, towing company, eatery, all the things that one man can do with a highway gas station and help from a hard-working family. It's run by the Kinskis, recent immigrants from Poland.

Paul Kinski was working in the garage when I got there. He laid down his wrench and straightened up to say hi. 'Got a job for you, Paul,' I told him. 'I'd appreciate getting it done right away.'

'What is it, Chief?' He wiped his hands and walked out with me to the cruiser. When he saw the damage he whistled. 'Somebody shot at you? What did you do?'

I raised one hand. 'It's a long story. How soon can you put it back together for me?'

He pursed his lips. 'Take a couple days. But if you don' mind driving with primer showing, you can have it back tonight. I can finish it in when you got time. I hear you're plenty busy.'

'Plenty busy. Can you give me a ride home if I leave it here?'

'There's just me on the pump,' he explained. 'Young Peter's gone to track and field. He's pole vaulting. For the school.'

'Good for him.' I'd have been more enthusiastic if his success hadn't interfered with my plans to grab some breakfast and a couple of hours' sleep.

'I can lend you a car,' Paul said. 'Jus' a little thing but it runs good.'

'It'll do me just fine until tonight. You're sure you can get this back to me by then?'

'Sure. Don't worry.' He flashed me a smile with gold in it. 'Come on, I show you the car.'

I stopped to get the shotgun from the front of the cruiser and stood and unloaded it, then stuck the shells in my top pocket and went after Paul to the fenced pound he keeps at the back of his place. He had a little red Civic running, and he got out and held the door for me. 'Six o'clock,' he said. 'Won't be pretty but you'll have a new window an' no holes.'

'Great. Thanks, Paul. I'll wait to hear from you.'

174

I got in and drove back into town, past the blackened bloodstain on the roadway where Langdon had died. All the locals had looked their fill by now and there were no cars around it.

It was only nine in the morning but Main Street was already buzzing. Cars were parked haphazardly all along the waterfront and up the road out of town. Visitors and people from the play production were moving about, the visitors tentative, the locals busy, busy, busy. I parked the Honda below the bridge, locked it and walked up the last hundred yards to the tent. Fred was inside, sitting in front of the stage with the baby beside her and Sam lying patiently next to her chair. When she saw me she excused herself from the people she was talking to and came over to give me a quick kiss. 'Hi, love. Hard night?'

I wanted to hug her and soak up some of her brightness and confidence but I just gave her arm a quick squeeze and said: 'Busy. I'm heading home for a while. I'll give you all the gory details later.'

'You want me to come up, get you something?'

I managed a laugh. 'The only thing you'd get me is excited and I need that sleep. Go on with the play. I'll see you later.'

'Thanks, dear.' She gave my hand a squeeze and I bent and talked to the baby for a moment, then left.

It was good to get to the house, back to normality. The garden was still neat. The willows still hung down over the water. The thin grass of my lawn still needed cutting and the porch still creaked when I stepped up to the door. Nothing in the framework of my life had changed because I'd left a tattooed little man dead in Veale's cabin.

Fred had prepared half a grapefruit and there was coffee in the pot but I didn't feel like either. Instead I got out my gun-cleaning kit and sat on the front porch with a newspaper over my lap, cleaning my revolver and the shotgun. It was hypnotic work, it is for any guy who was in the service. The crisp smell of solvents and gun oil, the routine of pulling through the barrel, wiping. Weary as I

175

was it took me back to the end of long hard days at Parris Island where I'd first learned how to care for guns. I worked for half an hour until everything was like new, then holstered my revolver, set the shotgun aside and sat for a moment looking out at the sunshine.

I must have drowsed because I started when a pickup truck pulled into the yard. Peter Horn, Jean's husband, got out and headed my way. I came down off the porch to meet him. He stopped to look at the garden, small-town courtesy, the business would come later. 'You didn't get the frost last week?'

'I covered everything up,' I said shortly. Politeness was fine but long chats on horticulture were low on my list of needs.

He straightened up and looked at me. 'Hear tell you found the guys't killed Jack McWatters an' the tourist. Shot two of 'em, one dead, one hurt. Other one got away.'

'Where'd you hear that?'

'On the radio. Figured it was right. Came to see how you were.'

'Tired, Peter. I got a couple of hours around supper time yesterday, otherwise I've been up two days and killed a guy.'

'You off now?'

'I'm taking a break, that's all.' He didn't say anything in reply and I prodded gently. 'Is there a problem somewhere?'

'Buncha guys is headin' up to Veale's, look for the other guy, Oliver. They figure he killed Jack McWatters.'

'I think the same thing, but I want him alive. Are they out to make him disappear?'

He inclined his head a quarter-inch. It meant the death sentence had been passed on Oliver.

'Listen, Peter. Don't let it happen. It won't solve anything. I'll have to go after them just the same as I have to go after Oliver.'

'Is a couple o' brothers o' Jack's. Been living in Sudbury, come home for his funeral. Them an' some others.'

'Have they left yet?'

'No. They're all over at Jack's house, talkin'.'

'Can you take me over there, Peter? The cruiser's in the shop having some bullet holes patched up.'

'Sure.' He nodded. 'Figured you'd come.' He went back to his truck and I went into the house for my cap and to stash the shotgun. Then I went out and got into Peter's truck.

As we neared the McWatters' house and saw the cars and trucks parked all around he said: 'His oldest brother is Cam, the other one's Will. I think you know everyone else.'

He pulled as close as he could to McWatters's house and I got out. The place was quiet, no music, no children playing, no TV. Peter got out of the truck and followed me up the path. I knocked on the door and waited.

McWatters's wife opened the door about halfway and stood so as to fill the rest of it. I touched my hat to her. 'Could I come in, Mrs McWatters?'

'For what?' She glanced back over her shoulder, nervously.

'I'd like to have a word with Cam and Will.'

Now the door was pulled wide open and a big man, lean and brown and fit, filled the space beside her, then pushed her gently to one side. 'I'm Cam McWatters.'

'I'm Chief Bennett, Murphy's Harbour police. Can I come in, please?'

A battle of staring began but I stood there, looking amiable until he realized I would stay all day if necessary. Then he stepped aside and I walked in past him.

There were half a dozen men in the room, all of them big, all Ojibway. Four of them were local band members; I knew them slightly and nodded to them then turned and extended my hand to the guy who'd let me in. 'I'm very sorry about your loss. I think I know who killed your brother and I expect to have him in custody really soon.'

He made no effort to shake my hand. 'Buncha white

guys gonna find him in the bush?' He drew his lips back in a sneer.

'They're trained men and they have a dog.'

'Retriever, right? When they shoot this guy, the dog brings him back, drops him at their feet.' He looked around, a grin on his face, the other men howled with laughter.

'They won't shoot him. They'll bring him in for trial. He'll go to jail.'

He had his back almost completely to me, laughing with the others. I saw the heavy knife in the sheath on the back of his belt. Then he spun back around to glare at me, his face twisted with anger. 'Trial? He kills Jack, cuts his heart an' you tell me about some whiteman trial.'

'We don't hang people any more. He'll get twenty-five years without parole.'

He laughed, hanging his mouth open and pushing his face into mine, his eyes as flat and hard as a frozen pond. I didn't pull away, even when he gave a quick thrust of his face, trying to back me off. His breath didn't have liquor on it. That much was good.

He stopped laughing now, dropping it like a clown mask. 'You won' need to lock him up. We'll bring him in, over a pole.'

'Do that and you'll serve the twenty-five years instead of him. That what you want?'

The others were quiet, watching Cam, their champion. As he went, they would go.

'We'll do what's right and who's gonna stop us?' he said in a menacing hiss.

'I am. Right here.' The room was silent. I made one last appeal for sense. 'If you want to go and look for him, fine, you can work with the OPP. You just don't hunt him down and kill him. This is a man we're talking about, not a moose.'

He straightened up, legs slightly apart, moving on the balls of his feet, his hand reaching around for his knife.

He spoke softly. 'This guy is dead. You got that. Now go home. You stay here you get hurt.'

He brought his hand around, holding his knife, a bowie style with a big blade, wide and sharp. He tossed it from hand to hand. He knew how to fight with it.

'Put that thing away before you get hurt.'

He laughed, from his mouth only, not his eyes, darting the knife at me in tiny thrusts. 'Not me. You the one who gets hurt.'

I backed up a half step and pulled my stick from my back pocket, drawing and throwing it in one gesture so it spun through the air at him like a propeller. He reacted instinctively, throwing both hands up to ward it off and I stepped in and kicked him a solid clunk in the shin. He gave a roaring groan, like the sound of some big sea mammal and dropped the knife, hopping on one leg as he held the injury. I stepped into him, giving him the elbow across the jaw and he sprawled backwards, out cold.

I bent to pick up his knife, then my stick. I slipped the stick back in my pocket and then turned to each of the men in turn, pointing at them with the tip of the knife blade. 'You do like I say. You work with the OPP or you stay here. Got that?'

Nobody spoke but the four local guys dropped their eyes. The other brother looked at me longest, then nodded. 'Awright. We'll stay here.'

'Good.' I tossed the knife up, catching it by the blade tip and handed it to him. 'Don't forget.'

Nobody spoke and I touched my hat to McWatters's wife who was standing against the stove and went out. Peter Horn was waiting on the step, expressionless. 'They changed their mind?'

'Yeah. Thanks.' I wiped my forehead with my fingers, they were slippery with sweat. 'Ran into a little trouble.'

'Settled now?' Peter led the way to his truck.

'I think so.' I got into the truck and yawned deeply. I saw the curtains flick at the McWatters' cabin. Someone had been watching, the yawn had been a good piece of theatre, showing how easily I'd taken care of business. 'I could sleep for a week,' I said.

Peter backed up and drove without speaking. When we'd crossed over the north bridge of our reach and were heading down towards my house he asked: 'You figure this guy's comin' here?'

'I wouldn't think so. If he can get out of the bush without the OPP finding him, it's my guess he'll head for Toronto. He's got money, he held up a donut shop, split sixteen hundred bucks with his buddy.'

'That 'merican had a roll thick as your wrist, I heard.' Peter gave me a sly little glance. 'He's got plenny o' money.'

'I'm not a hundred per cent sure he killed that tourist.'

He pulled into my yard with the unfamiliar little red car sitting there and switched off the motor. 'If he didn't, who did?'

Had it been anyone other than Peter Horn I would have clammed up, but Peter was the guy who took over for me on the rare times I got away for a vacation. He was almost a deputy. I trusted him. 'I still want to talk to the guy's cousins.'

'Hear tell they're church people,' he said cheerfully.

'They are. But I'm not sure they're telling the truth about the night Langdon was killed.'

Peter reached past me and opened the truck door. 'Get some sleep. Be easier then.'

'Thanks, Peter. If anything bad happens, give me a call.'

'I'll be in town,' he said and I knew he would be keeping his eyes open around my family. I slapped him on the arm and got out of the truck.

I showered and hit the feathers and the next six hours vanished. I woke to find Fred leaning over me. She grinned when I opened my eyes. 'It lives,' she said.

'It lusts,' I told her and reached up. 'Is the baby asleep?'

She nodded and I pulled her down to me. 'Whoa,' she whispered. 'I'm overdressed for this kind of exercise.' She wriggled out of her blue jeans and joined me and the whole wide world swam back into focus for both of us.

We lay there a while and she said: 'There's a couple of messages for you on the box. One from an Inspector Banner. He says you're reinstated.'

I kissed her, up in the edge of her hair. 'That's good. What else?'

'A call from the forensics lab in Toronto. Some guy called Gallagher.'

'Tony. Yes, we used to be in the Toronto department together. He joined the forensics outfit the year I came up here.'

'He says that the knife sent down by the OPP in Parry Sound had the blood of both victims on it – well, their groupings anyway.'

I gave her a last quick kiss and rolled my feet off the bed. 'Suspicions confirmed. Ready for a shower?'

Twenty minutes later we were down in the kitchen. Fred was wearing blue jeans and a pale yellow T-shirt with flowers on it. She looked beautiful. Me, I was doing the best I can with a shave, a fresh shirt and pair of uniform pants and a shoeshine. Sam was eating his dinner and he stopped and keened at me until I bent and patted his head. 'You're keeping him with you tonight, right?'

'Yes, boss.' She gave a mock salute. 'What would you like? A salad, a sandwich?'

'Whatever you say. I just live here. What were you going to have?'

'A cup of tea,' she said. 'It's opening night. I can't eat a thing.'

'In that case, let me take care of myself and you worry about Shakespeare.'

She winked at me and reached for the production notebook she had been carrying for months now. 'Thanks, love. I've got a couple of calls to make and I have to get back to the theatre.'

'What's happening with Louise?'

'She's going to be backstage with me. All our babysitters are in the cast.'

'That's good, as long as she doesn't get left out in the cold with nobody looking after her.'

'It's all worked out in scenes,' Fred said, reaching for the phone. 'I've cued it into each of their scripts. There'll be someone with her all the time.'

'Good.' I left her to her phoning while I made tea and cut myself a sandwich. I was planning my night's work as well. First to the station to check on the progress of the search for Oliver, then to round up the kid who had seen the Whelans at the bar and bring them together.

Fred spent the whole mealtime on the phone, then she woke up Louise and changed her into a pretty dress and loaded her into the car seat. I carried Louise out and strapped her into the seat belt of the car. 'I hate the theatre superstitions. I'd rather wish you good luck than bad. But if it has to be, then I'll do it the French way.'

'Sounds exciting,' Fred said.

I kissed her on the nose. '*Merde*.'

She held my arm, anxiously. 'You will be there if you can?'

'I'll be there for the curtain, I have promises to keep first. And someone has to be visible on the street to reassure the paying customers.'

'I know.' She reached up and kissed me quickly. 'Love you.' Then she put Sam in the back seat of the car, slipped behind the wheel and was gone. I waved to her, then got ready to work, bringing out the shotgun from the house and heading down to Kinski's to pick up the cruiser.

Main Street was a mess. The out-of-town ticket holders for the play had started to arrive and their cars almost blocked the roadway. Fred's helpers had done what I had asked, blocking off both ends of Main Street with saw-horses. She had installed a teenager at each end to let cars through so I was able to get by the front of the marquee and down to the bridge despite the flood of visitors pouring into the tavern and the Chinese restaurant and looking at the stalls of local handicrafts that Fred had organized.

No doubt about it, her work was paying off. This was

the biggest bonanza the town had ever seen. Everyone was benefiting, not just the merchants but the quilt-makers and woodcarvers and fly-tiers. All of them were doing business. And to top it all off, local charities would be getting the profits from theatre ticket sales. I was prouder than ever of Fred as I inched through. She had brightened up this town the way she had brightened up my life.

I got past Main Street and went straight down to Kinski's. As I passed the police station I glanced in and saw the local TV van with the cameraman and the reporter waiting for me and I groaned but kept on driving. I could handle that problem when I got to it.

Kinski pulled the cruiser out for my inspection. It had new side windows and the buckshot holes were all plugged but the area was covered with dull red primer paint. 'Best I could do in the time, Chief. Bring it back and give it me for two days it'll look like new,' he said.

'Looks great, thanks, Paul. I'll bring it back as soon as I can. Keep the tab running.'

He laughed. 'Don' worry. Maria keeps the books. She won' let you get away with nothin'.'

I laughed with him and drove back to the station. The TV crew sprang out to meet me, the camera focusing on the red-painted side of the cruiser.

Green eyes was ready with the question. 'Chief Bennett. Word is that you shot two men this morning.'

'I was in two firefights. In one I was attacked by a man with a shotgun. He missed me but hit my cruiser. Then later, at the same location, I was attacked by another man with a .308 rifle. He's in hospital in Parry Sound.'

They had the usual tangle of dumb questions. Including the dumbest of all. How did I feel?

'Do you really need to ask that?'

She wouldn't let go. Her voice was as shrill as fingernails on a blackboard. 'This is not the first man you've killed.'

'This is not the first man who has tried to kill me,' I said. 'Now I have work to do. This interview is over.'

She followed to the door of the station but I smiled politely and shut it in her face without speaking. She pounded on it for a couple of minutes but I ignored her, switching on the lights and checking the fax. I saw the cameraman filming me through the window but I ignored him and sat down to read my messages. By the time I looked up the pounding had stopped and the cameraman had gone away.

Banner had been as good as his word. There was a quick official memo stating that his investigation showed the homicide to have been justified and that I should not be suspended. I tore that one out carefully and filed it in the office day book. Later, when I'd finished with this investigation, I would catch up on all the paperwork.

There was another message, addressed to all police departments asking them to give special attention to all missing person reports. The woman who had been hijacked had not surfaced anywhere and so far her absence had not been reported. The same message described the evidence found at the bait drum in Veale's icehouse. The bloodstains on the exterior had proved to be human. They were not the same group as Veale, Corbett or Oliver, whose blood group was known from his prison records.

At this point in the fax messages I quit reading and rang Parry Sound and asked for the detectives. The desk man told me they were all out looking for Oliver.

'Up in the bush?'

He snorted. 'Hell, ain't you been reading the fax reports? He got outa there around noon.'

'I just came into the office. What happened?'

'He got by the guys who were lookin' for him. Got back to the camp. He cold-cocked the officer they'd left there. Hit 'im with the back of a hatchet. He was airlifted to Toronto. He's critical, got bad brain damage.'

I spent a few moments making sympathetic noises and then he gave me the rest of the news. Oliver had taken the four-by-four. It had been found twenty miles

184

south of Murphy's Harbour, abandoned in a parking lot used by people commuting to Toronto on the bus. So far there was no report of any vehicle missing from the lot but there was an officer checking with every busload of commuters that arrived. The last of them might not arrive until midnight. Until then it was assumed that Oliver was driving a car stolen from there.

I asked whether Veale had been questioned about the missing woman and the bloodstains on the bait drum. He had, but he had played dumb. He didn't know what the guys were talking about.

The desk man said: 'Hell of a way to get rid of a body, eh? Scattered all through the woods, picked up by wolves, bears, no two bones in the same place. We'll never find her.'

'The one we have to find is Oliver. He's a mad dog.'

The OPP man said: 'I'd watch my back, I was you. I heard from the guy at the hospital that Veale keeps saying Oliver's going to get you for killing his buddy.'

'He's got no idea who did that.'

'Don't you ever lookit TV?' The OPP man was astounded. 'Hell, it's all over the news that you killed him. Papers too, I bet, come morning. He's gonna know who did it and Veale says he was real thick with this Corbett. He's gonna come after you.'

'Thanks for the comforting words. If anything else comes in, please fax it to me right away.'

'Fer sure,' he said. 'You just watch yer ass.'

I hung up and read the rest of the faxes, including the report I'd just heard out loud. Oliver was top of everybody's hit parade. Great, I had a couple of hundred other cops helping to look for him. When he was found I could take a number and wait my turn to ask him about Langdon and McWatters.

On the face of it there was nothing to do but wait for that to happen. But I still had some questions for the Whelan brothers so I rang the kid who had seen their car at the Murphy's Arms. He wasn't in but his father said he would bring him down to the station for nine p.m. I rang the Bonanza Motel. The owner told me that the Americans were still there. 'That's four nights now. I've offered them a weekly rate if they stay till Tuesday.'

I headed up to bring them in. As I drove I rehearsed the way I would investigate. I would have to be gentle. It's not that I set much store by their religiosity. At best they'd be as honest as the next guy, at worst they would be hiding behind their bibles, expecting special treatment while they lied like horse thieves. No, the thing was that the media were sticking me with a reputation for brutality. It wouldn't take much of a squeal from a couple of churchgoers for me to be out of a job.

Their car and Langdon's jeep were both outside the unit. I knocked on the door and Langdon opened it. He stepped down when he saw me, closing the door behind him. 'Can we talk?'

'Sure. What's on your mind?'

He led me out a few steps from the doorway and I came with him, warily, anticipating a sucker punch. I knew he was an angry man. He stopped, at the corner of the building, and said: 'What's the story?'

'You heard me tell your cousins. They say they stayed here from the time Roy dropped your brother at the bar until I arrived with the news of his death. But I've got a kid who saw them at the bar after the fight. Why are they lying?'

'How good a witness is this kid?'

I looked at him, narrowing my eyes. 'You sound like all you're worrying about is could a good defence lawyer rattle him. What's the matter, don't you want your brother's death investigated?'

'What would it prove if they were down there?' He pushed the question at me impatiently.

'Let me talk to them and I'll find out. They're not accused of anything. They don't need a lawyer.'

He looked at me, then glanced away, out to the back

of the motel where the pines came down to the edge of the sparse, sandy lawn. 'They're my kin. Cousins.'

'And Thad was your brother. You blew into town blazing mad, swearing to find out who killed him. Now you're asking me to quit pushing the only lead I've got. What gives?'

He pushed his hands into his pockets and spat, a kid's action, self-disgust. 'They're nothin' but a couple dumbass ol' boys, raised without a father around.'

'It doesn't matter who they are. If they can help find your brother's killer I have to talk to them. So what if they lied about being down there, maybe they saw something valuable.'

He looked at me bleakly. 'Yeah. I guess you gotta talk to them.'

He led me back inside. The two brothers were sitting on one of the beds, side by side. Roy was reading aloud from the bible.

'The p'lice chief wants to ask you some questions,' Langdon said and sat down in the one chair in the room.

'We're ready,' Roy said. He closed the bible but kept his finger in his place, standing up.

'If you don't mind, I'd like to speak to you one at a time. You first, sir, since you're ready.'

He followed me outside. The sun was setting behind the pines and there was a golden tinge to the light, it felt religious, even to me, and I've stayed out of churches since Nam. Roy looked around him and sighed. 'Beautiful.'

I took the initiative back from him; if he could be saintly, I could be rough. 'Why did you lie to me about not going back to pick up your cousin?'

'It was my brother who told you that and what makes you so certain that he was lying?'

'Never mind the metaphysics, that's not my department. I deal in evidence. Somebody lies, I wonder why. Especially when two men are dead and a whole pile of money is missing.'

He concentrated on the sunset for a moment. 'Surely the man who killed Thaddeus took it.'

'I'm not here to fence with you. Are you interested in solving your cousin's murder or not?'

'Of course I am.' His voice dripped honey.

'Then tell me what you found when you went down to the bar looking for him.'

He frowned, a stagey gesture that made me more certain than ever that he was hiding something. 'I am not well versed in the law, but shouldn't there be a lawyer present while you ask someone questions?'

'That's when you've been charged with the murder. Right now we're just a couple of guys exchanging information. I've told you I know you were at the tavern at around the time your cousin was getting killed. You're about to tell me what you saw?'

'Even if I had been where you say, what could I have seen?'

'Which way did you drive home from the tavern? Did you go out along the road the tavern is on, or back over the bridge and out by the north road?'

He smiled a sad, sweet smile. 'Officer, why do you persist in claiming that we were at the tavern?'

'OK. Get your coat. I'm taking you and your brother to the police station to meet my witness. Then we'll talk.'

'This is most unnecessary,' he said sadly. 'Our poor cousin is killed and you persist in questioning us, two of the very few people who care about him.'

'This way.' I led him to the cruiser and opened the rear door. 'Inside.'

He opened his mouth to protest but I just pointed to the seat and he gave a shrug and sat in it. I slammed the door and went back to the unit.

George was still sitting on the bed, like a child waiting for his mother to see him off on a trip. He looked up at me and I told him: 'I'm taking your brother down to the station. You're coming too.'

He got to his feet without arguing and came to the door.

I looked at him closely. He was big, almost six feet tall and heavy-set, but there was a softness to him, a klutziness that explained why Langdon felt sorry for him and his brother. I realized that he would be the easier one to work on. Langdon was watching me, anxiously, not speaking. I said: 'Mr Langdon, could we have this room for a minute or so?'

Langdon got to his feet, looking at me carefully. He raised his right forefinger and waved it a couple of times, like a man beating time to music, a warning to go easy on George. I nodded to him and he walked out of the room.

'Sit down, please, George.' I indicated the chair Langdon had left. He sat, obediently, his hands in his lap.

'Which way did you drive home from the bar?'

'I don't know what you mean. I wasn't at the bar.'

He looked as innocent as a baby and I knew he would stick by his story as long as I acted tough. I took a deep breath. 'George, I haven't got the same faith as you have, but I know that there's a piece in the Gospels about rendering unto Caesar the things that are Caesar's.'

'Yes,' he nodded and smiled. 'Matthew, chapter twenty-two.'

'Well done.' I smiled back at him. 'Now I want you to understand that the information I'm asking for is due to the law, that's like St Matthew said only we don't talk about Caesar these days.'

His voice was high and light now, childish. He looked at me seriously and said: 'My brother said we should not talk about that night. It was too terrible.'

I sighed. 'Render unto Caesar, remember. Now, which way did you come home from the bar?'

For a moment I thought he was going to answer, then he shook his head. 'No. I promised Roy I wouldn't talk about that night.'

'OK. Let's go.' I touched him on the shoulder and he stood up. I opened the door and found Langdon right there. 'Mr Whelan doesn't want to talk to me. I'm taking him and his brother to the police station. I would appreciate it if you would drive their car down there, please.'

He nodded. 'Roy'll have the keys.'

I led them over to the car and opened the rear door. 'Can you let Mr Langdon have the keys of your car, please, sir?'

He frowned in a puzzled way then dug into his pocket and came out with a key ring. I handed it to Langdon who said: 'Thanks, Roy. I'll be right there with you.'

I put George in next to his brother and drove down to the station. Langdon stayed at the rear, pulling on to the lot behind me. I stopped and got out, leaving the Whelans in the cage. Langdon was getting out of their car and I said: 'I wonder could you oblige me by taking a look at what's in the glovebox and the trunk.'

'Help yourself.' He handed me the key but I shook my head.

'No, thank you. I have no official reason to search, I'm just curious, that's all.'

He shrugged and opened up the trunk. It was empty except for the spare tyre and a gas can. He picked up the gas can and looked around. 'Can't see anything.'

'How about the glovebox, please?'

He opened the passenger side door and sat on the seat while he checked the catch of the glovebox. 'Locked,' he said, and started searching through the keys on the ring. He found the right one and opened the box. The space was full of papers, maps, envelopes. He pulled them out in a sheaf and went through them quickly. 'Map, owner's manual, gas station coupons, muffler warranty –' He stopped suddenly and looked up at me. 'Jesus H. Christ on a crutch. There's an envelope here with a goddamn great roll of bills. It looks like Thad's money.'

14

He counted the money. 'There's forty-two hundred an' eighty dollars here,' he said softly.

'And that looks like a bloodstain on that top bill.' I held out my hand. 'If you were to pass that money over to me as evidence, I'll be able to complete the investigation of your brother's death.' I was skating down the edge of the law and I wanted to stay on the clean side. If he didn't help me I would have to do things the hard way, with no chance to use this money as evidence. He hesitated so I went on: 'You'll get it back when the investigation is complete.'

He pushed the bills back into the envelope and handed it to me without a word. I took it to the police car. Roy was twisted around in his seat, looking back at me. When I opened the door on his side he said: 'That money belongs to our cousin Thaddeus Langdon.'

'I'd like to hear all about it. But first, would you and your brother please come into the station with me and I'll advise you of your legal rights and then we'll talk.'

'Of course.' He was gravely calm. 'Come, George, let's go with the officer.'

Langdon was still standing off by their car and he suddenly slammed the door and shouted: 'How could you do it?'

Roy turned back to speak to him, his voice calm and low. 'We did not harm Thaddeus. It was the other gentleman we hurt.'

I took them into the back of the station and sat them

down on either side of my interrogation desk. Langdon stayed outside for a couple of minutes, then banged on the side door and I let him in.

By the look of it he had been weeping. His face was chalk-white and he leant back against the wall and folded his arms while I spoke to Roy. 'I personally saw this money in Mr Langdon's possession on the night he died. You have told me that you didn't come down to the bar after you dropped him off, that means he didn't have access to the car you are driving, not from the time I saw him until his death.'

Roy was following but I was going a little fast for George who frowned at me nervously. I went on, anyway. 'Somebody took his money and put it into the glovebox of your car. At this time I am not charging you with his murder, nor with theft, just with possession of stolen money.'

Roy nodded gravely. 'It is right that I should be arrested.'

'OK, Mr Whelan. Stay there, please, I'll get the tape recorder.'

They sat in silence while I got out the office Sony, stated the date and time, their names and the charge, read their rights again and let Roy talk.

'I am a man of peace. May God forgive me for what I did.'

'And what was that, exactly?'

'My brother and I were worried that Thaddeus would be drinking to excess. So we came to the tavern to look for him.'

'And what happened?'

'We saw signs that there had been some kind of disturbance in the bar. Thad wasn't there so we left, driving back by the other road to the highway.' He paused and smiled at me, vacantly, 'Like the Magi after they spoke to Herod and went on to see the Holy Infant.'

I waited and he went on. 'And we found Thaddeus and another gentleman fighting. As we drove up, the other man seemed to punch Thaddeus in the chest and he stopped fighting. He put both his hands to the place he had been hit, and then we saw that he was bleeding.'

'What did the other man do?'

'When we stopped the car he came towards us, shouting, and I saw that he had a knife in his hand and the blade was dull with blood.'

'And then?'

'Then we got out of the car and he waved his knife at my brother and I threw a stone that I picked up from the shoulder of the road and it hit him in the temple.'

'Like David and Goliath.' I headed off his reference. 'And then what did you do, Mr Whelan?'

'And then I really sinned.' He stopped speaking for a moment and rolled his eyes to the ceiling, moving his lips silently.

I waited until he had finished then prompted. 'Could you tell me exactly what you did, sir?'

'I looked at Thaddeus and saw that he had been stabbed. And I was angry and forgot my teachings and went back to the law of the Old Testament.' His voice was rolling and liquid, I could imagine him in a glittery suit on television, hounding the faithful for donations to further the works of his ministry.

'I need to know exactly what you did, Mr Whelan?'

'I picked up the knife the other man had used. I could see that it was Thad's own knife, the one he had carried when he hunted the bear. I supposed that this other man had taken it away from him.'

Again, his lips worked silently for a moment but I did not prompt him, he was on a roll here, he would talk. At last he cleared his throat and went on: 'I could see that the other man was sorely hurt. I thought he would die of the injury I had caused him with the stone. I was afraid. We were in a strange country and I had killed a man. And so I covered up what I had done. I stabbed him in the chest as he had stabbed Thaddeus. I thought that the police would think the same man had killed them both.'

'And then what did you do?'

'Then we put him into his truck, which was still running

193

and I drove it up to a deserted house and put his body in the water.'

'And how did you get away from this deserted house, you call it, where you left him?'

'My brother drove our car and he picked me up and we went back to our motel and prayed.'

'And what about the money that your cousin was carrying? It was found in your car. How did it get there?'

'I took it. I was going to give it to the poor.' Roy dropped his head down until his chin was on his chest. 'Believe me, Officer, I am not a thief.'

'Is there anything you wish to add to what you've told me, Mr Whelan?'

'I would like to say that my brother George played no part in what happened. It was I alone who killed the man and drove him away. And may the Lord have mercy on me for what I did.'

I let the tape roll for ten seconds more then said, 'Interview ended at eight-twenty-two p.m.,' and switched it off.

Langdon came away from the wall in an angry rush. I stood up to protect Whelan but he stopped short of hitting him. 'You sonofabitch,' he hissed. 'Gonna give the money to the goddamn poor.' He threw his arms up convulsively. 'You didn't think of his mother. She ain' rich. But you didn't think of her, did you? You were gonna buy your way into heaven with Thad's money.'

I made a hushing gesture and spoke quietly. 'You'll get the money back, Mr Langdon. It's needed for the trial, that's all. And these men didn't kill your brother, they did their best to defend him.' Hell, what a day, I thought, start off in a firefight, end up pleading for mercy for a murderer.

He clenched his mouth shut until he had control of himself then walked away a couple of steps, stretching his facial muscles the way cooks do when they're chopping onions. 'What happens now?'

'They'll be kept in custody, pending a court appearance. If you'll wait a few minutes, I will give you a receipt for

194

your brother's money. Then you'll be free to go, but we'll need you back here for the trial.'

He was on the point of tears but he shook his finger at Roy Whelan. 'I'll see your sorry ass in court,' he said and went through to the front office to wait for me.

I stood the Whelans up and searched them then took their belts and shoelaces and locked them up in separate cells. They did not speak, except for Roy who asked if he could keep his bible. I let him take it with him and once the door was locked on his cage he began to read aloud. I listened for a moment then went through to the office and wrote out a receipt for Langdon. He nodded and took it then asked: 'Will you have their car put in your pound?'

'Yes. Why don't you head home right away. I'll notify you when they come to trial.'

He nodded his head slowly. 'Those dumb bastards. God. I hate 'em.'

'Pity them. They're going to find out about hell first-hand when they get to jail.'

He nodded again, not speaking, and I said: 'I'm sorry you had to come to our town this way. Sorry it's ended up like it has. Don't go away thinking we're all a bunch of bastards here.'

He said nothing, didn't even look my way, just walked out of the door, shutting it quietly.

I sat there for a while after his car drove away, then phoned Parry Sound OPP. There was a different inspector on duty, a self-important dummy I've had trouble with in the past. He listened to my report and just grunted.

I took a deep breath and went by the book. 'This call is to notify you that the homicide cases at Murphy's Harbour are closed. I want to thank you for the generous assistance that has been given to my department by the OPP and am formally cancelling my request for help.'

'And in the meantime you've shot two people and I've got more men than I can spare out looking for your suspect.' He was on his high horse and I had to listen.

'They're searching for Stuart Oliver, wanted for a rob-

195

bery and rape at the donut store in your bailiwick and for attempted murder of one of your officers. When they find him, tell them not to bother booking him on my behalf.'

'He's also wanted for abduction of a woman and possible murder.'

'I know, Inspector. I'm the man who tipped you off on that case. Can I speak to your desk man now?'

The phone clattered down and the desk man picked up. I was lucky this time, it was a sergeant I knew. His first words were: 'Nice goin', Reid. What I heard, you solved both homicides.'

'Thanks, Frank. Listen. I've got the two suspects in my cells. I can't baby-sit them all night, the town's full of visitors for the play on Main Street. Any chance you can send the wagon down to take them to the regional detention centre?'

'Can't spare a wagon, but I'll contact Watson, he's on patrol south of the Harbour, he can take them in.'

'Great. I'll be here when he comes, thanks a bundle.'

I hung up and phoned the witness I had asked for the nine o'clock line-up. His father was disappointed that it wouldn't be happening. I guess he'd been counting on having a war story for the guys at work.

When I'd got him off the line I went in to check on the Whelans. Roy had set the bible aside and was leading a prayer session. They were both kneeling beside their bunks, eyes closed while Roy wove his spell. I left them to it and went back to the office, spending a pleasantly numb half-hour typing out the charges against them. Manslaughter, causing indignity to human remains, theft of money, obstructing police. A good lawyer, even a Legal Aid guy would plea-bargain it down to the manslaughter charge and they'd get off with five years, less for George, he'd been a bystander. But jail would be tough for them. I didn't get any satisfaction out of thinking about what would happen to them inside.

The OPP cruiser got there just after nine and I shipped them off with him. Then I shut the money and the tape recorder into the office safe, closed up and headed for Main Street.

I got there at the play's intermission. The audience had spilled out of the tent and were relaxing outside, against the water's edge. A few were smoking but most were sipping soft drinks that Fred had arranged for. They were being sold by kids she couldn't find onstage work for. She'd thought of everything.

I found her backstage, working with the cast. She was playing Titania, dressed in a filmy costume with wings and wearing stage make-up, what she called her warpaint. She was busy and I stayed out of her sight while she passed on her notes to the cast. They didn't notice me either, all of them were totally involved with their acting. Carl Simmons was standing, in his costume smock, with the big papier-mâché ass's head under his arm, all his usual sophistication gone as he listened to Fred's directions as intently as any of the others. All of them were totally wrapped up in their parts. This was the most exciting night of their lives, another gift Fred had given the town.

Louise was asleep in her car seat next to her baby-sitter, a teenager in some kind of green elf costume. She was reading her script intently. Sam was lying beside her and he saw me and keened in his throat. That caught Fred's attention. She turned and smiled distractedly and I made a little gesture for her to continue. When she'd finished she came over and asked: 'Did you just get here?'

'Yes, I'm sorry, I haven't seen anything of the play. I've been busy. I've got the homicides solved. Two men in custody.'

'Brilliant.' She beamed like the sun and gave me a quick kiss. 'Would you like me to make an announcement when the play is over?'

'No. This is your evening. Keep it that way. I'm proud of you.'

'You're a dear thing,' she said. 'But listen, can you not take Sam with you now everything's all right? He's having a lousy time back here with everyone coming and going.'

197

Oliver was still on the loose but I was going to be close by from here on. 'Sure thing,' I said. 'Turn him over.'

She went to Sam and knelt beside him, the Fairy Queen, freeing him from his spell. 'Go with Reid,' she told him.

He squirmed with delight and wagged his tail as I fussed him while a guy with a stopwatch spoke to Fred. 'Right. Give them the five-minute warning,' she told him and he went through to the stage, carrying a big school bell. It clanged twice and Louise stirred and woke. At once the sitter was on the job, talking softly to her, unclipping her harness and lifting her out. Then Louise saw me and held out her arms. I took her for a moment, until she was properly awake and able to go back to the sitter. Then I clicked my tongue at Sam and went out and around to front of the marquee.

The last of the audience was trailing in. From their comments it sounded as if the play was a success. No big city critics had turned out to shred the performance by comparing it with the best of Broadway, these were people on vacation, looking for a pleasant night out. And they'd found it.

Once the action started again I was alone outside except for some of the kids who had been selling the drinks. Three of them walked down to the bridge and lit up. They only had one cigarette between them so it wasn't hard to figure out what they were smoking, but I ignored them. One joint wasn't going to bring down the government.

Another boy and girl stood together at the water's edge, talking softly, holding hands. Their own drama had a lot more going for it than anything Shakespeare could offer. I strolled into the back of the audience and watched the players. Carl in particular was very good as Bottom. He and Fred had collaborated on adding a few contemporary lines to the text, making fun of current fads and institutions. I hit the scene where he's asking a fairy to bring him wonderful food and he included an order of tofu. The audience roared. I figured Shakespeare would have approved.

I took a hard look at the stage lights. Working in a tent makes it difficult to set them up properly. The local electrician had done his best, stringing most of them almost directly over the stage, where the pitch of the tent was at its highest. They looked safely strung, but I'd had his work vetted by the fire department and they had given him a grudging passmark. 'As long as the tent stays up, you're fine,' the captain had told me. 'Just keep your eyes on those guy ropes.'

With that warning in my mind I didn't linger in the tent. I went back out and took a slow patrol around, checking all the retaining ropes. Everything looked fine and I walked back along Main Street, checking the parked cars, idly, not really expecting trouble. The TV van was parked close to the bridge, carefully placed to make a quick exit after the show. They had come to town to record the play, I figured, their interview with me earlier on had been a freebie, something to do until the curtain went up.

There was a sudden roar of laughter from the tent and I looked back to where it glowed pale orange against the dark of the trees beyond. And as I watched, the top of it canted slightly to the left.

'Seek!' I shouted and Sam bounded ahead of me towards it. He ran to the right, around the back of the tent. I went the other way, hearing his working snarl before I reached him, and found him crouching and baring his teeth in front of a man with a knife.

'Fight!' I shouted and Sam grabbed the man's knife hand. He swore and tried to change hands but I grabbed his other wrist and spun him around, forcing him to the ground. 'Lie still or the dog'll tear your arm off,' I hissed and he gave a groan and stopped struggling.

I told Sam, 'easy' and he backed off a foot while I snapped the handcuffs on the man's wrist. Then I levered him up by the arms, and turned him around so I could see who it was.

'Doug Wilson. What's with the knife?'

He just swore and I remembered the way the roof line

of the tent had jogged. 'You cut the guy ropes. You sonofabitch, you could kill somebody in there.'

'Serves 'em all right,' he whispered. 'They screwed my wife.'

'Come on.' I grabbed him and forced him along the side of the tent until I came to a cut rope. I unlocked one side of the handcuffs so he could put his hands in front of him. 'Grab that rope and pull till your arms break.'

'Or what?'

'Or you're in jail for attempted murder. Do it.'

He hesitated a moment, then pulled on the rope with all his truck-driver strength. I slipped the cleat and took up the slack until I had enough to tie the cut ends together in a sheetbend. Then I put my own weight into the pull, alongside him until we had the roof line back to where it was.

'Good. Come with me.' I led him along past the front of the tent. The kids who had been standing around had come back, curious about why I had run so fast. They whispered together when they saw Wilson. Word had gotten around fast that he'd been stuck with the horns.

I marched him to the cruiser, then took the other handcuff off him and sat him in the cage. He didn't offer any resistance, just sat there, staring ahead, blindly. I went back to the tent, stooping to fuss Sam who was frisking at my side, glad to be working again. 'You're a good cop,' I whispered to him. 'Come on, let's find the knife.'

Sam led me right to it, a good-quality kitchen knife with a ten-inch blade. That was bad. It meant Wilson had thought this thing through in advance. He hadn't just taken out his pocket-knife and impulsively slashed the rope, he had gone home and picked up the knife and walked down the road to the tent with the definite plan of bringing it down on the people inside. He hadn't meant to murder anybody, maybe, but there could have been deaths from fire, or from panic.

I took the knife with me and opened the front door of the cruiser to talk to Wilson. 'Did this come from your house? Or did you buy it on your way up here from Toronto?'

'What's it matter? I wanted the goddamn tent to come down on all of them.'

I glanced about me. The kids had gathered around, as close as they could come without drawing attention to themselves. I couldn't talk here. I clicked at Sam and he jumped into the car then I got in and drove down the road past the bridge. I stopped there, out of sight of the kids and turned around to talk to Wilson through the mesh of the cage.

'If that tent comes down, people will die.'

He didn't answer but he wiped his eyes with his shirt-sleeve.

'Is that what you want? Is it going to change anything about your marriage?'

'What marriage?' He sniffed and wiped his eyes again. 'We're getting a divorce.'

I sighed. Life can be complicated, even when there's no crime involved. 'Look, I'm not a marriage counsellor but I don't think that's a good idea.'

'What would you know?' He was in control of his voice now.

'I know a lot about people. Your wife is a good woman. She's even more upset about what happened than you are. If she wasn't, you'd never have found out because she wouldn't have made up the story.'

His anger suddenly flared. 'That slimy little bastard. I'd like to break his goddamn neck.'

'If it makes you feel any better I kicked his ass good last night.'

'Naah.'

'Yeah. This is between us, all right? It goes no further.'

'Sure. I wanna hear.'

He did. He wanted it to have been *his* boot. He wanted to feel the impact right up his own leg. So I obliged him.

'He was trying to keep the rapist story alive so he phoned my office and told my wife he was going to rape her. When I sorted out what had happened I just lost it. He must have gone two foot up in the air.'

He laughed, then choked it off into a snort. I waited and after a while he said: 'Look. What I did was dumb, Chief. I won't do anything like that again, I promise.'

'If you do, I'll have to throw the book at you, you know that.'

'I won't,' he said. 'I wanna go home, talk to Amy.'

I turned the car and headed back up to the bridge and let him out. He reached out his hand to shake. 'Thanks, Chief. I've been a dork.'

We shook and I slapped his shoulder and he left, walking briskly past the tent and up towards his house. I called Sam out of the car and went over to lean on the rail of the bridge. Things were working out.

From the tent there came another wave of laughter. Fred was doing a hell of a job, all the months of work and worry paying off. I was glad. She was too big and bright a character to be fulfilled in a town this size unless she could make a contribution this important. She had mentioned once, in the winter, that she wanted to run for local council. If she did it after tonight she would win in a landslide.

That thought made me start considering the current council and my own status with the reeve. He was beaten now. With the rape case and both murders solved I would be almost as much of a star as my wife. Hell, what a team.

I stood for a while, listening to the roar of the falls beneath the bridge, then walked slowly down to the tent to see the end of the play. I was looking forward to the excitement of the players afterwards, the compliments, the laughter, and then to heading home with my wife and baby with everything in the world rosy. I was about as content as a man can be.

I sneaked a peek through the back flap of the tent. A crowd of offstage actors were there, along with one girl who was holding Louise and talking to her. Everything was under control, but I left Sam outside the door with the order to 'keep'. None of the cast would be coming out and he would stop anyone from going in. If he barked I could come around and check who it was.

There was a ticket collector at the door of the tent and he bobbed his head at me and let me past. I went in and stood at the back of the seats. There were a couple of other people standing, but I didn't recognize them in the low light. I concentrated on the play.

Over the months of Fred's involvement I had come to know the play pretty well and I recognized that this was close to the end. Puck was alone on stage. By day he was a clerk in the grocery store. Tonight he was Laurence Olivier as he declaimed his last speech but one. He came to the line that goes: *'Now is the time of night, that the graves all gaping wide, every one lets forth his sprite,'* when I felt a nudge in my ribs. I turned my head but a man's voice said, 'Don't try nothin' fancy, this is a gun. Just walk outside like we're the best friends in the world, OK?'

15

There are no rules in martial arts for dealing with a gun in your back. You do as you're told, period.

I turned and walked out. I widened my eyes helplessly at the kid on the door but he was stagestruck, watching the play, his lips moving silently with the words. Useless.

The pressure stayed in my back, square on my spine. If the bullet didn't kill me it would put me in a wheelchair for life. I kept walking, away from the tent towards the bridge. The kids who had been standing around were all gone, there was nobody on Main Street but the two of us.

'Right. This is good.' He prodded me with the gun barrel, no doubt now, I could feel it through my shirt. It was steel. He unsnapped my holster and took out my service revolver. 'OK, now turn around real slow,' he said.

I did. He had stepped back one pace, out of reach of a sucker kick. 'I reckon you know me,' he said.

'I reckon I do, Stu.'

'Yeah. You an' everybody in the world's got a fuckin' TV.' His voice was soft. 'Worse'n America's Most Wanted. Everybody in the world's after my ass.'

I tried inching back another full stride, seven or eight feet from him and it would be worth the risk of a dive out of his way. From this range it would be suicide. He moved forward the same amount. 'You can't get away. I'm going to shoot you in both knees, and then in the gut.'

'Not the best idea, Stu. Everybody will come pouring out. You can't kill all of them.'

'I won't need to. They'll run 'n hide when they see the gun. An' you'll still be here wishing you was dead.'

He laughed suddenly. 'Hey, I got an idea. We can make your wish come true. Back off.'

I backed off, moving fast but he moved at the same pace. 'Slower, one step at a time, back to the water.'

I glanced over my shoulder. The water's edge was forty feet from me. I could also see a vehicle of some kind pulling on to the bridge from the far side, driving slowly.

'Lookit me,' Oliver commanded. 'I'll tell you how far.'

I had a chance now, slim but possible. When I got close enough I could dive into the water. If I hit it before he could pull the trigger I might make it. A chance. I concentrated on calculating how close I was to the water.

He followed, step by step, keeping the same distance between us as I backed up.

'Can you tell me what this is all about?'

'You know what it's about.' His voice was low, I had to strain to hear. 'It's about my friend Murray. You shot the poor little bastard.'

'He shot at me.'

'Should've hit you in the guts,' he said. 'Should've left you layin' there wishin' you was dead.'

'He nearly did it. I was lucky.' There was still only five feet of space between us and I was still ten feet from the water, too far to dive.

'Hold it there,' he said. 'I can throw you in from there when I've shot you.'

'What good's that gonna do?'

'None. That's why I'm gonna do it.' He laughed and gestured with the gun. 'Not feelin' so good now, are you? We're not talkin' about some poor little bastard scared of the dark. We're talkin' about me an' what's really gonna happen.'

'Look,' I said and gestured at him, covering up the fact that I'd stolen a half pace back.

He jammed the gun towards my chest. 'Put your hands up.'

I raised my hands, racking my brain for a plan, a chance. All I could think was to keep backing to the water's edge, and dive. But he was going to shoot if I did, I couldn't get away with it.

He lowered the gun in his left hand until it was pointing at my stomach. 'Take a minute to think about it,' he said. 'You'll be shot, in the water, not knowing whether to drown or die. An' I'll be gone. I'm gonna give you a countdown and then shoot. OK?'

'Look, it doesn't have to be this way. You can get away.'

'Nine,' he said. 'Eight.' He opened his mouth wide, grinning like a skull. I was too far to grab the gun so I tried a last desperate trick. I pretended to vomit and as I made the strangling sick noise he backed away a half step, distracted and I dived aside, tugging at my stick.

The muzzle flash lit up the night. But he missed. I rolled again and came up with my stick in my hand. Not much against two guns but the threat of it would spoil his aim if he shot again. He turned to face me. In the blue light from the marina his face was a grinning mask. He raised his left hand and I threw my stick and broke to my left, hoping to reach the shotgun in the cruiser before he could hit me.

And then everything went into slow motion. He suddenly checked, as if he'd been cramped. Both hands with the guns in them sagged to his sides. Then his knees folded and he dropped the guns and reached for his chest and I saw a dark circle spreading there.

I darted forward and kicked his gun aside, grabbing my own and holding it on him and whistling for Sam.

He came galloping around the tent but before I could give him a command, Oliver keeled over and lay on his side and I saw that blood was pouring from his mouth.

I crouched beside him, fingering the bloodstain in his chest and then I understood. The head of an arrow was projecting through it, on a line with his heart.

206

People were crowding out of the play tent now, but one man was running towards me, carrying something ungainly in his right hand. It was Langdon. 'Sniper shot,' he said, holding up the crossbow in both hands. 'Right through the heart.'

I stuck my hand out to him. 'Thank you. The last time the army did this for me was in Nam.'

'Nam.' He shook my hand. 'You old guys are all the same. We won my goddamn war.'

Behind me a woman screamed. 'Officer! This man's hurt!'

I gave Langdon's hand a quick double handshake. 'Stay, please. I have to work right now.'

'Sure.' His voice was almost drowned out by more screams. I turned around and went back to work to clean up the mess.

Everyone I needed was in the audience. Dr McQuaig checked Oliver and pronounced him dead. Les McKenney walked the two blocks to his business and came back with the hearse. And the reeve and all the councillors were there to see what police work can look like close up. There was even a TV crew, the persistent couple from Parry Sound, to record Oliver's body lying there with an arrow sticking through it, and Walter Langdon looking like a latterday Robin Hood.

The whole cast had come pouring out, in costume, and they were mingling with the civilians so that the TV tape became a hot commodity that played all across the country on prime national news. Langdon, of course, was a star, which suited me just fine. He had sure as hell earned it in my book.

In the end he stuck around for a week with Fred and me and the baby while the OPP did its investigation and cleared him, giving him a civilian citation for his work. He was there for the first hearing on his cousins when they were held over for trial in October.

And maybe the biggest winner was the town. People flocked in from all over Canada and even places in the

States when the TV tape was played. In a shaky summer, when the economy was still fairly feeble, we had the biggest tourist year on record, and *Midsummer Night on Main Street* ran for three whole weeks.

The only downside to the whole operation was that the Wilsons moved away. Murphy's Harbour is a small town and we have our share of small-town minds and small-town gossips and things got uncomfortable for Amy at school. But they stayed together, which was the important thing. And the young couple who bought their place are both anxious to get parts in Fred's next production. She's not waiting for next summer. Stay tuned for *A Winter's Tale*, in the Legion Hall as part of our Ice Carnival next January. But don't expect Fred in the cast. Louise is expecting a brother in April and Fred's staying offstage until after that.